"What if I want you to stay?" His husky tone played havoc with her senses.

She took a fortifying breath. "Forgive me for being blunt, but I can't afford to stay." *I'm far too attracted to you.*

How could she feel this strongly about him when it hadn't been that long ago Ferrante had died? She didn't want to know the pain of loving someone again, and was shocked at the strength of her feelings for him already. A prominent man like Stavros Konstantinos could have his pick of any woman, but he could never be serious about *her*. It wasn't worth risking her heart to stay around any longer—especially when she'd be leaving the country with her father in the not too distant future.

Dear Reader,

I once worked for a tour agency, and loved writing the itineraries for various groups.

One in particular was arranged for a well-known opera singer who would come on a tour and take his group to the cities where he'd performed. Paris, Milan and Zurich were among the high points of his tour. I wanted to add Athens, Greece, but the singer had time constraints so it didn't happen.

Greece is one of the most fascinating, amazing countries on earth. If I could have planned a Greek itinerary for him I would have included the island of Thassos. When you read this novel you'll see why.

Enjoy!

Rebecca

THE RENEGADE BILLIONAIRE

BY
REBECCA WINTERS

First published in Great Britain 2015
by Mills & Boon, an imprint of Harlequin (UK) Limited,
Eton House, 18-24 Paradise Road, Richmond, Surrey, TW9 1SR

© 2015 Rebecca Winters

ISBN: 978-0-263-25758-8

Printed and bound in Great Britain
by CPI Antony Rowe, Chippenham, Wiltshire

Rebecca Winters lives in Salt Lake City, Utah. With canyons and high alpine meadows full of wildflowers, she never runs out of places to explore. They, plus her favourite vacation spots in Europe, often end up as backgrounds for her romance novels, because writing is her passion, along with her family and church.

Rebecca loves to hear from readers. If you wish to e-mail her, please visit her website at: cleanromances.com

Books by Rebecca Winters

Mills & Boon® Romance

The Count's Christmas Baby
A Marriage Made in Italy
The Greek's Tiny Miracle
At the Chateau for Christmas
Taming the French Tycoon

Princes of Europe

Expecting the Prince's Baby
Becoming the Prince's Wife

Gingerbread Girls

Marry Me Under the Mistletoe

Tiny Miracles

Baby out of the Blue
Along Came Twins...

Visit the author profile page at millsandboon.co.uk for more titles

To my wonderful children, who put up with me while I write books of the heart. They know I love them, but they also know my mind is often somewhere deep into a love story of my own concoction.

CHAPTER ONE

AFTER WASHING THE sweat from his body, Stavros Konstantinos wrapped a towel around his hips and walked out on his terrace. The view of the blue Aegean from his private villa atop pine-covered Mount Ypsarion always renewed him.

Because of another of many such impasses, today's board meeting in Thessaloniki on the Greek mainland had ended early for him. His proposal for a new product to be manufactured and marketed by the Konstantinos Marble Corporation had met with total defeat.

At that point a blackness had swept through him. The sickness that had been coming on for the past year had finally caught up to him. Depression was a feeling he'd never known before, but he couldn't label it as anything else.

Knowing that his family members who made up the majority of the board still lived and operated as if it were 1950, he hadn't expected any other result. With the exception of his elder brother, Leon, everyone else down to the last cousin was against any new innovations and refused to hear him out. They were afraid of change.

That was fine with him. In his free time he'd had a new plant built on his own land. Now that the family had refused to listen to him and wanted no part of it, he and his two partners, Theo and Zander, would be starting production on Monday.

Since he'd gotten nowhere with the members of the board, he'd told them he was resigning from his position as managing director of the corporation immediately. As of now, all ties were severed, including his position on the board. He suggested they should start looking for a replacement ASAP.

Just saying those words helped to drive some of the blackness away. He'd been in a cage, but no longer.

While every member sat there in utter shock at his announcement, he excused himself from the meeting in Thessaloniki and took the helicopter back to his villa on Thassos Island. En route, he checked his phone messages and discovered another text message waiting for him from Tina Nasso, the woman he'd stopped seeing three months ago.

Since he'd never responded to any of her messages, why would she text him again? Was she so desperate?

This separation from u can't go on, Stavros. You've been so cruel. I haven't seen u or even heard your voice in three months! You haven't texted me back once. I have to talk to you! This is important. Tina.

This text meant she was still pressing for him to change his mind. His black brows came together. Christina Nasso, the woman his parents had expected him to marry, didn't know how to let something go that could never have worked out. With no intention of answering this text either, he deleted it.

Parental pressure had driven him to spend some time with her, but there was no attraction on his part. He had the gut feeling her parents were still pressuring her because they'd wanted an alliance between both families. Just as his parents had planned on him marrying her, it was no secret the prominent Nasso shipping family from Kavala wanted Stavros for their son-in-law. Both family businesses were closely connected.

But when she'd wanted a deeper intimacy with him, he couldn't pretend feelings he didn't have. Though he hadn't wanted to hurt her, he'd had to tell her the truth. He wasn't in love with her and they both needed to be free.

Stavros had told his parents the same thing after they'd demanded an explanation. His great mistake was humoring them from the beginning. Never again. They could wait, but a marriage with Tina wouldn't happen.

Today he'd felt the consequences of his actions. His refusal to go on seeing her had caused a serious rift, one he'd felt at the board meeting when his father had influenced his uncles and cousins to close ranks against his new business venture instead of embracing it.

As for Tina, his hope was that one day she'd meet someone her family would approve of. She was an attractive woman with much to offer a man who wanted to marry her. But Stavros wasn't that man. One day, Tina would realize it and move on. Like salt that had lost its savor, every relationship he'd had with a woman had been missing the essential ingredient for happiness.

The only thing that brought him any pleasure right now was spending every bit of time on his new business. Stavros's company wouldn't be in competition with his family's, but there would be fireworks when they found out he'd gone ahead with production. One of theirs was doing something on his own and they couldn't tolerate it. But it shouldn't be a surprise to them. He rarely bowed to the dictates of his autocratic father or his great-uncles.

For his mother's sake, he'd tried where Tina was concerned. But once she'd learned that her younger son wasn't enamored of the Nasso girl, he'd found disfavor in her eyes too. He took a deep breath. Today had turned out to be a day like no other. From here on out, his life was going to go in directions no one would be happy about except him.

So be it!

On his way to the kitchen to quench his thirst, his cell phone rang. If it was Tina calling because he hadn't answered her text, she would find out exactly how he felt when she realized he intended to go on ignoring any and all phone calls or texts from her.

But when he looked at the caller ID, he saw it was the manager of quarry three on Thassos Island phoning on his private line. He clicked on. "What's up, Gus?"

"Kyrie Konstantinos?" *Kyrie* being the Greek version of Mr. "A situation with one of the student-teacher groups from PanHellenic Tours has arisen. A teenager is missing. Now the police are involved."

This was all Stavros needed to hear, especially

since he'd been the only one on the board in favor of allowing tour groups to visit the quarry. The program had been working well since March with no incidents, until today...

Stavros gripped the phone tighter. "Have the police started a search?"

When he heard the particulars, he grimaced. A helicopter would have an almost impossible struggle to see any movement beneath the dense green canopy of the forest.

"What do you advise, Kyrie?"

"I'll be there ASAP."

He returned to the bedroom and dressed quickly before he dashed out the door to his car.

It had been his hope the quarry experience would broaden the students' education and spread the word about job opportunities.

Forty percent of the marble in Greece came from an almost inexhaustible supply in the Thassos region, much of it being shipped to China, Asia and Europe. Because of this abundant natural resource, more jobs were available, which would improve the Grecian economy, a major aim of his.

With that argument, his grandfather, who'd recently passed away, had been persuaded that the free publicity generated by various tour groups from foreign climes might be a good idea. At that point the rest of the board offered their reluctant acceptance on the condition that it would be for a trial basis only. One problem with the tours and they'd be given no more access.

This particular quarry—one of many owned by the family throughout northern Greece—was on the other side of the summit, just ten minutes away. He knew the police lieutenant well and would ask his cooperation in keeping the press at bay for as long as possible.

The crisis needed to be averted before the media got hold of it. Once they turned it into an international circus, the island would be crawling with unwanted spectators. Though the staff at the quarry wasn't responsible for what had happened, the public wouldn't see it that way. Publicity of this kind was never good.

To his mind, the teacher was ultimately responsible for this type of situation and could be facing charges. Six high school groups of six on the bus with their individual teachers? How hard was it to keep track of half a dozen students?

Gus had said the teen's teacher was a younger, nice-looking American woman. Maybe too young to handle a bunch of teens? Stavros pressed on the gas as he rounded a curve in the road. He was in a mood.

Once the family found out about this crisis, they'd put a stop to the tour groups. Since he'd announced his resignation from the corporation and the board, he would no longer have a say. But for the time being he felt the responsibility heavily. Someone's teenage son was missing in a foreign land and needed to be found.

Panagia was Andrea Linford's favorite village on the Greek island of Thassos. After flying from Thessaloniki to the nearby airport of Keramoti on the mainland, she'd come the rest of the way on the ferry to Thassos, the capital city many referred to as Limenas. From the water, the island looked like a floating forest because of the pines and olive groves covering it.

She'd rented a car and driven to Panagia, ten kilometers away. Named after the Virgin Mary, it was built on the side of the mountain. From the wooden terraces of the villas with their painted ceilings and schist roofs, one had a fantastic view of the bay and the sea beyond, where other emerald-green mountains rose to fill the eye. The sight of clear, ice-cold water bubbling up from the natural springs to run down alongside the narrow streets delighted her.

Andrea had spent time in its church of the Virgin Mary, which had been built in 1831. She loved its impressive baronial style, constructed by stones from the ruins of ancient temples. The exterior and cupola were a pale blue and white, absolutely exquisite.

She'd been in a lot of churches around the world, but the interior of this particular church was like a fabulous treasure. It contained a banneret dating from the time of the Crusades. She felt there was a spiritual essence she hadn't found in other churches. If she were ever to get married, this would be the spot she would choose, but of course that was a fantasy, just like the village spread out before her.

Today she didn't have time to linger.

For the past year and a half, Andrea had worked for PanHellenic Tours, in their main office located in Thessaloniki. They were one of the biggest tour operators in Greece. Having obtained her humanities degree from the university there, she had been hired to do translations and help develop tour itineraries by researching everything thoroughly.

Andrea was the person who'd first suggested the company include a tour of the quarry she found fascinating. Her boss, Sakis, was so taken with her idea, he'd made it part of their latest itineraries for this year. But word had gotten back to him that there'd been an incident involving an American student visiting the marble quarry on Thassos. The boy had gone missing and the police had been called in.

Because Andrea was fluent in English and Greek, and because she'd been the one to make the initial arrangements with the quarry manager, Sakis had sent her to do the troubleshooting, then report back her findings.

Before leaving the office in the cotton skirt and blouse she'd worn to work, she downloaded the student's file, including a picture, and itinerary on her phone.

Knowing the way to the quarry, which was famous for its pure white marble, she left the charming island village shaded by huge oak and walnut trees—a village that maintained some of the old traditions and ways of life. She followed the road up the mountain.

Thassos was truly an emerald island, almost round in shape. Some of the locals called it a giant lump of marble. She smiled as she wound around until she came to the quarry.

Many of the stone mines scattered all over the island were open pits. A tourist who didn't know better would think they'd come across an enormous, surreal graveyard of huge, pure white marble slabs and blocks surrounded by dark green pines. They glistened in the hot late-afternoon August sun.

She made her way to the quarry office of the Konstantinos Corporation, a world leader in the production of marble from their many quarries in northern Greece. Thanks to large investments in technology, the company processed marble and granite for internal and international markets.

At the east end of the quarry, she saw the tour bus and half a dozen police cars parked by the employees' cars. The officers were obviously vetting the group of students and teachers standing outside it.

She parked her car on the end of the row and got out. Georgios, the seasoned Greek tour guide, was a harmless flirt who always made her smile when he came to the head office, but today he looked grim, with good reason.

No sooner had she gotten out of the rental car to talk to him than the police lieutenant approached her. "Sorry, but no visitors are allowed here today."

"I've come from PanHellenic Tours," Andrea said in Greek. She introduced herself as a representative of the tour company and showed him her credentials. Normally she wore the blue jacket with the PanHellenic insignia, but it was too hot out.

"My mistake."

"No problem. Our office received word that one of the American students, a seventeen-year-old named Darren Lewis, disappeared during the tour of the quarry and hasn't been found. I'm here to help if I can. Any news yet?"

The mustached lieutenant frowned. "A helicopter has been making a sweep of the mountains. Some of the officers are out searching the area for him, but so far there's been no word."

"How long has he been missing?"

"Almost three hours. All the quarry employees have been accounted for. None could shed any light and were told to keep this quiet. We're about finished getting statements from the students and teachers. Then they're free to go on to their next stop in Thassos."

Three hours… It had taken her too long to get here. By now the dark blond boy could be hiding anywhere in these mountains. Thankfully, with the eighty-degree temperature, it wouldn't get too cold tonight, if he wasn't found by dark.

"Before they leave, I need to talk to the tour guide."

"Of course."

"Excuse me."

She hurried over to Georgios, the short, wiry Greek who knew this business backward and forward. "This is a ghastly thing to happen. How are you holding up?"

He shook his head. "I've been with the company for fifteen years and never lost anyone before. After the tour had finished, the quarry manager said the group could look around. You know the routine. I told them to be back at the bus in a half hour. Darren told his teacher, Mrs. Shapiro, that he needed to visit the restroom before heading for the bus."

"That's when he gave her the slip?"

"So it seems."

"She must be as devastated as you are."

He nodded. "We did a head count when everyone got on the bus, but he was missing. One of the students who had sat by him remembered he was wearing his backpack while they toured the quarry."

"In this heat you wouldn't want to be hampered by a backpack without good reason. It sounds like he might have had a plan before he ever arrived here," she theorized.

"That's what the police think too. I'm inclined to agree with them. The group knows to leave their belongings on the bus during an excursion, but it wasn't a hard, fast rule. After this experience, I'm going to insist on it. That is, if I don't get fired."

Andrea shook her head. "Sakis knows this isn't anyone's fault but Darren's," she assured him. But she knew how the public would react. Anyone and everyone would be blamed. "According to the file, he isn't on any medications, but that doesn't rule out the possibility of his taking recreational drugs. What's he been like?"

"Throughout the tour, his behavior didn't stand out one way or the other. His teacher says he's an honor student, somewhat on the quiet side." He scratched his head. "His parents have to be notified."

"I'll report back to Sakis and he'll take care of it if he hasn't already. Right now you've got a group of hungry, thirsty students and teachers who need attention. Go ahead and get them on board. I'll catch up with you later and help you any way I can."

"Thanks, Andrea."

She turned away just as a black Mercedes sedan suddenly appeared out of nowhere and drove right up, blocking her path. A tall, dark-haired male with a powerful build alighted from the front seat with an aura of authority that couldn't be denied. The man, maybe in his early thirties, was so ruggedly Greek and gorgeous, her mind went blank for a minute.

Before she averted her eyes to keep from staring at him, her gaze took in the lime polo shirt and light khaki gabardine pants. His clothes only emphasized his hard-muscled body. He wore a gold watch, but no wedding band and looked as expensively turned out as the gleaming black car he drove. Andrea had no idea such a man existed. Where had *he* come from?

"Kyrie Konstantinos!"

The lieutenant's exclamation, plus his show of deference, answered her question. This stranger with black hair swept back from a visible widow's peak had to be one of the men whose family owned and ran the internationally renowned corporation.

He shook the lieutenant's hand. "After the plant manager told me the news, I got here as soon as I could. Tell me what happened." The two men discussed the situation and talked about keeping this incident from the press while the search was ongoing.

Between impossibly black lashes, his dark gray gaze swerved to Andrea. For a heart-stopping moment, she was subjected to a thorough, faintly accusing male scrutiny of her face and body that made her go hot and cold at the same time. To have such a visceral reaction to a man she'd never met stunned her.

He broke off talking to the lieutenant and moved toward her. Switching to English, he said, "I take it *you're* the American teacher who was in charge of the runaway teen? How was it possible he disappeared on your watch?"

He'd fired the question with only a trace of accent. That didn't surprise her given his affluent background and education. What did surprise her was the fact that he'd correctly assumed she was American. Something about her had given her away. Furthermore, it seemed he'd decided that she was the teacher in question, the one whom he'd already tried, judged and convicted as the guilty party without knowing all the facts.

Andrea expected the lieutenant to step in at this point and explain, but his attention had been diverted by one of the officers. It was up to her to clarify the situation before he made any more erroneous assumptions.

"I believe introductions are in order first," she answered in Greek. "My name is Andrea Linford. I'm a representative of PanHellenic Tours in Thessaloniki. My boss sent me out to be of help to the tour guide, Georgios Debakis, and offer any assistance before I return to the office with my report."

She held out her hand, which he was forced to shake. His firm grip tightened a little before he released her, but she felt the imprint of his hand travel through her whole body and stay there. There it went again. That shocking sensation from just being in his presence. To fill the disturbing silence since he hadn't spoken yet, she said, "Which Konstantinos are you in the hierarchy? Leon, Stavros, Alexios or Charis?"

More silence ensued before he muttered, "Stavros." She'd studied the facts of the company on the way here and remembered that Stavros was managing director of the Konstantinos Corporation. "You've done your homework, Kyria Linford."

"Despinis," she corrected him. She wasn't married.

"My apology for misreading the situation."

His apology had been difficult for him to verbalize, but she would cut him some slack. "You were half-right. For all my sins, I am American. But I'm not poor Mrs. Shapiro, who no doubt you assumed didn't have the maturity to handle a group of teenage students away from their parents. If I'm wrong in that assumption, then *my* apology."

His intelligent eyes flickered with some unnamed emotion. "You weren't wrong," he admitted in his deep voice.

"Thank you for your honesty. I think we can both agree this is an ugly situation all the way around and no one is at his or her best. My boss is beside himself. He has to make the call to the teen's family and explain that their son is missing. Hopefully they'll supply him with a reason why he might have run off midtour."

"Let's hope he's found within the hour."

She nodded her blond head. "We all want that. Unfortunately, his disappearance happened on your company property and will put the Konstantinos name in the spotlight, bringing you adverse publicity. As for poor Mrs. Shapiro and Georgios, they'll be in agony until Darren's found."

He raked a bronzed hand through his gleaming black hair. "I asked the lieutenant to keep this quiet for as long as possible."

"I heard you. Let's hope one of the officers doesn't leak it for a while. That boy has got to be found!"

Her voice shook because she was remembering the long ten-day wait before her fiancé's dead body had been spotted on the mountain ledge, dashing her dreams for their marriage. The thought of Darren's parents having to wait that long for any news made her shudder, a reaction Kyrie Konstantinos observed while he studied her.

She tore her eyes from his in time to see the tour bus drive out of the parking area to the road. Her heart was heavy for the teacher and Georgios, who had to keep doing their jobs while they were dying inside. Andrea felt anxious over the situation too. Where *was* Darren?

"With only a three-and-a-half-hour head start, he can't get too far." The incredibly handsome Greek read her mind aloud.

Andrea folded her arms to her waist. "Did you know he has his backpack with him? I wonder if he'd been planning his escape long before today in order to survive while he was on the run."

"If so, he picked the right spot. It's true these mountains will give him cover and the forest is dense, but I've lived here all my life and know every inch of ground. If the search and rescue teams don't find him, *I* will."

Stavros Konstantinos instilled such confidence in her, Andrea had no doubts he could do anything. She was alarmed by her thoughts about him—considering he was a stranger, she shouldn't have been thinking about him at all. "You'll need his description and a picture. I can email the information in his file to your phone right now."

He pulled out his cell and gave her his number. Within a minute, he'd received it. She watched him study the dark blond boy's passport photo. "He's nice looking with that Marine cut. It says he's five-eleven with brown eyes. He'll be easy enough to recognize."

"Unless he was carrying a disguise in his pack. Maybe turn himself into a woman?"

He flicked her another searching glance that sent a curl of physical awareness through her. "That would definitely throw anyone looking for him off the scent. I'll pass your idea on to the lieutenant in case he hadn't thought of it. You never know.

"Perhaps you noticed Darren's birth date on the passport. He turned eighteen yesterday, which makes him an adult."

"I didn't catch that." This man's mind was a steel trap.

"What else do I need to know about him?"

She sucked in her breath. "My boss found out Darren comes from a well-to-do Connecticut family, so he probably has enough money on him to last for a while. Maybe he planned this before leaving the States, possibly with someone else who's waiting for him at another destination."

"Anything's possible."

"My guess is he'll try to leave the island by boat rather than ferry. I've been studying my map of Thassos. There are dozens of harbors. How hard would it be for him to pay a fisherman to take him somewhere else and escape under the radar, so to speak?"

His eyes narrowed on her features. "It sounds like you've had experience with this kind of thing before."

"Some," she admitted. But not while she'd been working for the tour company.

"If he tries to get away in a boat, the harbor police will be onto him. In the meantime, I'll head back to my house to change and go after him. As I recall, your tour brochure mentioned the Dragon Cave near Panagia."

"Yes. They would have toured it this morning."

"Then he might have decided to go there to hide for the night."

"You're right." She hadn't thought of that. "You'd make an excellent detective if you hadn't been born a Konstantinos." The comment had slipped out of her mouth before she could stop it. What in heaven's name was wrong with her?

After a pause his lips twitched. "There's a thought." His amused tone played havoc with her breathing.

Andrea had visited the Dragon Cave months ago. It contained amazing stalactites and stalagmites. She'd seen the stalactite shaped like a dragon. "The literature says the cave hasn't been fully explored." Fear clutched her heart to think Darren might be foolish enough to penetrate a danger zone.

"I'll check there first. There's no time to waste."

"Kyrie Konstantinos—" She thought he was about to walk away and wanted to stop him. He eyed her with such a penetrating gray gaze, she felt he could see right through her. This important man was ready to drop everything to look for a boy he didn't know. With the police already doing a search, he didn't have to do it and no one would expect it of him.

On top of his overwhelming male attributes, there was a goodness in him she could feel. The combination startled Andrea. She felt drawn to him in ways she couldn't explain and would have to analyze later. "I'd like to go with you and help."

He looked stunned. "Why would you want to get involved?"

"Because in a sense this is my fault. I'm the one who asked the quarry manager if we could bring our tours here. These quarries have been worked for a thousand years, yet many tourists still aren't aware of their existence. I find them fascinating and convinced my boss to agree to the idea of a tour here in the first place."

His head reared back in surprise. "*Your* idea?"

"Yes. I can only imagine how much you wish your quarry manager had said no to me. I realize everything is a risk, but you could have no idea how responsible I feel now that this has happened on your company's property. And to be honest, there's another reason..."

She felt his gaze travel over her. "What would that be?"

"Eighteen months ago I lost my fiancé. He was a mountain-climbing guide who'd gone up on Mont Blanc with some other climbers. They were caught in a terrible storm. When it was discovered he was missing, I was told I couldn't assist in the search because it would be too dangerous."

"I'm sorry," he whispered. Immediately, his eyes softened with compassion. She could feel it.

"I had to wait ten agonizing days until they found his body on a ledge. When I think of this boy's parents hearing the news that their son is missing, I can't stand by and do nothing." Her eyes smarted with unshed tears. "Even if I'm not able to do any good, I want to help in the search for him."

She heard him inhale sharply. "You can add me to that list of people who feel responsible because *I'm* the person Gus appealed to for permission to allow tours here."

A small cry escaped her lips. "I knew he would have to go through channels. What a surprise to find out it was *you*." Incredible.

"I'd say today has brought several surprises. But I don't regret giving permission, not even under these circumstances."

She took an unsteady breath. "Neither do I. Hundreds of students and teachers have benefited from what they've learned here."

"That's been my hope too."

His words warmed her. She sensed he was a man she could trust. It was her own unexpected attraction to him she didn't trust. "Whatever the outcome, please don't worry that you'll be liable. The tour company will take full responsibility."

In the silence that followed, she took it to mean he *was* thinking about a possible lawsuit from the boy's family once their attorney found out the Konstantinos family's worth was in the millions. She wouldn't blame this man for having no use for today's litigious society. It was also apparent he wasn't keen on her help.

Disappointed that she couldn't be of help, she started to walk around his car to get to hers.

"Despinis Linford?"

Andrea whirled around.

"You're welcome to come with me. But we could be out all night."

All night alone with him? Her heart thudded for no good reason— except that wasn't true. She knew exactly why it was thudding. She wanted to be with him. "I don't care about that. If we can find Darren, that's all I ask."

"Then we'll have to go back to my house for a few provisions."

"Thank you. I'll follow you."

She got back in the rental car. En route, she called her boss and told him what was going on. Then she phoned Georgios and explained that she was going to help in the search for Darren and would keep in close touch. He thanked her in a shaken voice before they hung up.

The fact that Darren was now eighteen meant he was no longer a minor. Maybe his parents had given him this tour for a birthday present. To Andrea, his disappearance was more troubling than ever. As an adult, he could do what he wanted.

Andrea didn't think she could handle it if anything happened to him before he was reunited with his parents. It hadn't been that long since Ferrante's death. Being hired by PanHellenic Tours had saved her life and she was doing better these days. But Darren's disappearance triggered remembered pain from that terrible ten days when she'd waited for word.

CHAPTER TWO

THROUGH THE REARVIEW MIRROR, Stavros watched the rental car following him to the house. Andrea Linford had come as a complete surprise in so many ways; he was still in mild shock. Her Greek was amazing, but there was a lot more to her than her linguistic ability.

When he'd first laid eyes on her, he'd jumped to the wrong conclusion. To his chagrin, the first words to come out of his mouth had been accusatory. But she'd turned the tables on him with that very maturity he'd thought had been lacking. Over the course of a few minutes, he'd found himself utterly overwhelmed by the unexpected strength of his feelings for her.

The fact that she wanted to help find a boy she'd never met revealed a depth of character that appealed to him. For her to confide her agonized feelings to Stavros over the death of her fiancé—to have felt so helpless while she'd waited for word of him—it had torn him up inside.

The shocks kept coming. Since she'd been the one to plan an itinerary that included a tour of the quarry, she must be a person who thought outside the box. He found that intriguing.

As for her physical attributes, those long legs and

the way she moved her shapely body had branded her
an American. She was a natural, honey-blonde beauty
with deep, sky-blue eyes who needed no makeup to
be attractive.

No wonder Gus hadn't been able to turn her down
when she'd approached him on behalf of PanHellenic
Tours. She'd probably had that same effect on her
boss, who couldn't help but hire her.

Hell. She'd had that effect on *him* or he wouldn't
have agreed to let her come along to search for the
boy. Talk about a day like no other!

When he reached the house, he pulled around the
back next to his Jeep. She parked on the other side of
him. He tried not to stare, but he couldn't help glanc-
ing sideways when she got out of her car. In an odd
way, her sensible walking shoes only drew more attention to those beautiful legs of hers,

"Come in the house and freshen up in the guest
bathroom while I gather a few items. I'll pack some
food and drinks so we can eat along the way."

"Let me help."

Once inside the rear entrance, he showed her
where to go before he loaded up a food hamper in
the kitchen. With that done, he walked through the
house to the bedroom to change into jeans and a crew-
neck shirt.

After checking with the police lieutenant, who had
no good news to report yet, Stavros pulled on his hiking boots, then drew some parkas and sweaters from
his closet. On the way back to the kitchen, he stopped
in the storage room for his large flashlight and extra
batteries. A smaller flashlight was in the Jeep.

His soft top was loaded with everything else they

might need: blankets, a small tent, a bedroll, a couple of fold-up camp chairs and extra petrol. He was always prepared in these mountains. Whether they found Darren tonight or not, they'd be comfortable.

Stavros had never taken a woman camping with him. It was going to be a novel experience. He realized he was looking forward to being with her. When he'd walked out of the board meeting for the last time earlier in the day, little had he dreamed that by nightfall he'd be searching for a runaway teen with this lovely woman.

When Andrea saw him coming, she relieved him of the coats and sweaters so he could carry everything else. They left the house and hurried out to the Jeep. By the time they were packed up and ready to go, twilight had fallen over the lush landscape.

He started down the road toward another one that would lead to the Dragon Cave. "Did you talk to your boss?"

"Yes. He's already informed Darren's parents. They'll be on the next plane to Thessaloniki."

"Could they shed any light concerning their son?"

"No. He's a scholar who'll be attending Yale in the fall. They're baffled and in agony.

"Sakis told me not to come back to work without the boy. That's how anxious he is."

"We'll find him."

"Since this is your backyard, I believe you."

Her faith in him was humbling. "How about digging in that hamper for a couple of sandwiches. My housekeeper makes them up for me."

"Sure."

She turned around on her knees and reached in the

hamper behind his seat. Her movement sent a faint flowery scent wafting past his nostrils, igniting his senses, which had been in a deep sleep for longer than he cared to remember. After handing him one and taking one for herself, she pulled out two ice-cold bottles of water.

They rode for a few more minutes before she asked, "How high up are we?"

"About four thousand feet."

"That's high for an island. Have you climbed to the top of Mount Ypsarion?"

"Many times." He darted her a glance. "Have you ever climbed a mountain?"

"Yes. Mount Kilimanjaro."

At her unexpected answer, Stavros let out a whistle. "That's over nineteen thousand feet high."

"I found that out when I needed to stay on the oxygen above fourteen thousand feet. My dad took me up while he was working in Tanzania."

Fascinated, he said, "Does he still work there?"

"No. From there he was sent to French Guiana for two years, then India for three. Later he spent two years in Paraguay and another two in Venezuela. From there he was sent to the Brusson area of northwestern Italy for three years. Then he came to northern Greece. We live in Thessaloniki, where I got my degree in history and archaeology from Aristotle University."

Stavros marveled. "What does your father do?"

"He works for W.B. Smythe, an American engineering company in Denver, Colorado, where I was born. Gold practically built the state. His company designs and fabricates modular plants and equipment for the extraction of gold and silver. As of this year, they've established a global presence in twenty-four countries. From the time I was born, I've lived with my father wherever he was sent." He'd be going to Indonesia next.

"How many languages do you speak?"

She let out a sigh. "Besides the obvious, I'm fluent in Italian and French, and speak some Hindi, Afrikaans, Swahili, Spanish and Guarani. It's no great thing. You have to learn a country's language while you're there if you hope to survive. Lucky for Darren, a lot of your countrymen speak English."

"Amen." He cleared his throat. "What about your mother?"

"She died giving birth to me."

He smothered a moan. *No mother...*

"Dad and I have been nomads, traveling the globe. He was the one who taught me about the white marble quarries here."

The feminine fountain of knowledge sitting next to him was blowing him away. Everything about her had already gotten under his skin. "What exactly did he tell you?"

"Besides the fact that the quartz crystalline structure resembles freshly fallen snow and is only quarried on this island?"

"Besides that."

"He passed on a piece of trivia I found interesting. The visual effects team working on the American films of the *Twilight* saga used very fine pure white Thassos marble dust, which they added to the face paint. That's why there's this incredible sparkling effect when sunlight touches the vampires' skin! Trust my dad to know details like that. He's the smartest man I ever met."

Stavros filed the information away. "Have you told him that lately?"

"All the time."

"Lucky man." Since Stavros's father already believed he was the smartest man living, Stavros had never paid him such a compliment.

"I'm the lucky one to have a father like him."

"You know what I think?"

She flicked him a curious glance.

"Despinis Linford is the smartest woman *I* ever met."

"Hardly." Another troubled sigh passed her lips. "Please. Call me Andrea."

"Then I insist you call me Stavros."

"The sign of the cross. A holy name."

"My parents regret giving it to me. I'm afraid I'm the *apololos provato* of their brood."

She turned her head to look at him. "You? The black sheep of the Konstantinos family? Why would you say such a thing?"

"Maybe because I choose to do things other than live up to my father's dreams for me."

"It sounds like you have dreams of your own and think for yourself. There's nothing wrong with that. You ought to wear it as a badge of courage rather than a curse."

A curse. That was exactly what it had been like, but she made it sound like something to be proud of. A different way to look at himself? How did she manage to do that without even being aware of her power? The thought was daunting because he realized he could really care about her. That was a complication he didn't need right now.

"You're fortunate to have a father who approves of you."

"You mean yours really doesn't?"

"Afraid not." His voice grated. "Your incredulity tells me how different our fathers are. In my whole life, we've rarely seen eye to eye on anything. Unless it's his way, it isn't right."

"But you're obviously successful!"

"Not in his eyes."

"That's horrible." Her voice shook. "How painful for you."

"I'm used to it."

"Even so, I can hear the hurt in your voice deep down." Her keen perception astounded him. She studied him for a minute. "For what it's worth, I approve of you."

"Why?"

"When we first met, you were ready to give me a full interrogation at the quarry. But after I introduced myself, you listened, and in your unique way, you apologized and let me look for Darren with you. I find that admirable and think I like you much better now."

Andrea Linford, where did you come from?

Little did she know he already liked her to the point he was ready to carry her off to an unknown location where they could get to know each other for as long as they wanted, undisturbed by anything or one. It shocked him that he would entertain such a thought when he'd only just met her.

They'd neared the trail that led to the cave. It was

getting too dark for tourists to be out. Stavros had been watching for anyone walking along the winding stone road bordered by heavy underbrush.

He pulled to a stop. "We'll have to go on foot from here. Grab one of the parkas. I know it'll drown you, but it will also keep you warm. The temperature inside the cave is always cooler, especially at night. Darren might not be here. If he isn't, then let's whisper once we get inside while we wait and turn off the flashlights. In case he does show up, we don't want our voices and lights to scare him off before we approach him."

"Understood."

Andrea understood about a lot more things than he could have imagined.

They both got out and put on a coat. She reached for two bottles of water she could carry in the pockets of her parka.

He handed her the smaller flashlight, making sure it worked, then turned on the big one. After throwing a blanket over his shoulder, he locked the Jeep. Before he knew it, she'd gone down the path ahead of him. Because of the overgrowth of mountain foliage, it grew so narrow in spots that they had to proceed single file. So far, they hadn't seen anyone.

Soon, they came to the large mouth of the cave. It looked like a dark hole. He moved past her, flashing his light around the interior for any sign of the teen. They went deeper, until the shaft of light lit up the dragon-like stalactite. Though it was always dark in the cave, the night gave it added menace.

If Darren intended to hide in here, Stavros doubted he'd go much farther for fear of getting lost. He turned to Andrea and put his lips close to her ear. Again, he was assailed by the delicious scent of her. Maybe it was the shampoo from her wavy dark blond hair, which fell loose to her neck. "Let's sit here awhile and see if he comes."

Andrea nodded and edged away in order to counteract the feel of his warm breath against her skin. He hadn't touched her, but he didn't have to for her to be intensely aware of him. After he spread out the blanket, she sat down cross-legged. In the next moment he'd taken the same position facing her.

The last thing she saw before they turned off their lights was the bone structure of his striking eastern Macedonian features. He was fiercely male, *all* of him.

Just thinking about all of him made her swallow hard. She felt the cool darkness enshroud them. If she was nervous and disturbed, it wasn't because they were in a cave that was black as pitch. Something had happened to her from the moment Stavros Konstantinos had alighted from his car looking like a Greek statue come to life. It was so strange because she hadn't been interested in any man since Ferrante.

"Do you know what a rare creature you are?" His whisper came out of the darkness.

Her body trembled in reaction. "Why do you say that?" she whispered back.

"Because your behavior is so perfect, you've forced me to break the silence in order to tell you so."

Andrea couldn't help but smile. "I learned early in life that most men don't like chatter. Of course, my father isn't like most men. I loved him and always wanted to go with him wherever he was sent."

"Is he waiting for you in Thessaloniki?"

"No. He stays in a village near the Skouries mine for three weeks at a time. Then he comes to our furnished apartment in the city to see me for a week. While I'm at the office, he cooks up a storm for us. I take time off when he arrives so we can explore the sites together."

"Your father never married again?"

"I once asked him that question because he's had his share of girlfriends. He told me that because he has to move around the globe every so often, he decided it would be too difficult to be married. Plus, he said, I was the only child he wanted."

"I can understand that. Both his reasons make perfect sense. Would you have liked a stepmother?"

No one had ever asked her that question. "I don't know, since I never grew up with my own mother. To be honest, I didn't care for some of his girlfriends and they didn't care for me, so I'm glad he didn't marry one of them."

She could hear a change in his breathing. "How old are you, Andrea?"

"Twenty-six. And you?" she fired back, growing more curious to know everything about him.

"Thirty-two. Tell me about the man you were going to marry."

He'd changed the subject fast.

"Ferrante was Italian-Swiss from Ticino. He came from a large family with five brothers and sisters of whom he was the eldest. I've never met anyone so happy and friendly. Some people have a sunny spirit. He was one of them."

In the silence that followed, a warm hand reached

out and found one of hers to squeeze. "I'm sorry you lost him."

His sincerity reached the deepest part inside her, but Andrea wished he hadn't touched her. Still, she didn't pull away because she didn't want to offend him when he was trying to give her comfort.

"I'm much better these days. What about you? Do you have a girlfriend?"

He removed the hand that had spread warmth through her body. "Like your father, I've had my share."

"But so far you've stopped short of marriage."

"Yes."

"That *yes* sounded emphatic," she observed. "With a last name like yours, I guess you can't be too careful."

"Your perceptiveness must be a gift you were born with."

"I think it's the influence of my rather cynical father."

"So he *does* have one flaw..." His response sounded almost playful. "I was beginning to worry."

"Why?"

"A perfect father is hard to live up to."

"Are we talking about mine?"

She was waiting for his answer when she heard a faint noise. Andrea supposed it could be a rodent running around, but she hoped it was Darren and jumped to her feet. In the process, her body collided with Stavros, who was also standing, and he wrapped her in his strong arms.

"Don't make a sound." This time his lips brushed

her cheek while he whispered. Instantly rivulets of desire coursed through her bloodstream.

While she stood there locked against his well-honed frame, there was more noise, a little louder than before. Whatever made the sound was getting closer to them. Stavros must have been holding his flashlight because he turned it on in time to see a ferret scurry away.

Andrea relaxed against him, but Stavros still held on to her. No longer whispering, he said, "It's past eleven o'clock. If Darren had planned to come here tonight, he would have arrived by now, don't you think?"

She eased out of his arms and turned on her flashlight so he couldn't tell how much his nearness had turned her body to mush.

"I do." Until she got herself under control, Andrea wasn't capable of saying anything else.

"Since the lieutenant hasn't phoned me with news yet, that means Darren's still out there, but I doubt he'll do any more hiking before first light." He scooped up the blanket and folded it. "Since he's not here, it's possible he took the trail leading away from the quarry that eventually goes down the mountain. There are firebreaks that crisscross it. We'll take one, then another. Hopefully we'll locate him."

"That sounds like a good plan." Together they left and made their way back to the Jeep. The slightly warmer air outside the dank cave felt good, but she kept the parka on. Once they'd climbed inside, he started it up and they took off at a clip. He turned on his brights to help them in their search. Andrea drank some of her water, thankful he knew where to drive.

"Are you hungry, Stavros?"

"Another gyro sounds good."

She turned around and got another one out of the hamper and handed it to him. He'd also packed some plums, so she took one for herself and settled back to eat. "Seeing Thassos Island in the dazzling light of day isn't anything like driving through this forest at night."

"Not so benign, is it?"

A shiver passed through her. "No. Wherever our runaway is, he couldn't be feeling as comfortable about his plan right now. My boss checked with the American consulate. Darren has never been issued a passport before. Since this is his first trip to Europe, it's amazing he'd be willing to run away from the tour in a place so foreign to him. He has to be desperate."

"Or adventurous and headstrong," Stavros suggested, "and too spoiled to realize how hard this has to be on his parents or anyone who cares about him."

She had a hunch he was talking about his younger self. "We have to find him before the press turns his disappearance into an international incident."

"You took the words out of my mouth." His voice sounded an octave lower and resonated to the marrow of her bones.

At the first crossroads they came to, he braked and turned right. "While I drive slowly, shine the big flashlight into the trees. We'll take turns calling out his name. If he's hurt and needs help, he might show himself."

"That's a good idea, but if he wants to stay hidden—"

"Then the sound of our voices will make him nervous that people are looking for him," Stavros supplied. "Hopefully he'll try to run and in the process give himself away."

For the next half hour, he drove them over one rough firebreak, then another. "There doesn't seem to be any sign of him, Stavros. Do you think it's possible he hid himself in one of the employees' vehicles while no one was paying attention? Maybe the back of a truck or the trunk of a car?"

Andrea noted the grim expression marring his arresting features. "Those are the first places I assumed the police had looked before I got there. But if they weren't thorough enough…" His voice drifted off.

"Do all the workers live nearby?"

"Their homes are in or around Panagia. If that's what Darren did, then he could lose himself among the tourists in the morning."

Andrea nodded. "With enough money, he could buy a bike or steal one. Once in Thassos, he could take the ferry to the mainland."

For the second time that night, Stavros clasped the hand nearest him. "Who should have been the detective now?" Heat passed through her system in waves before he let it go. "I'll find us a place to camp on the outskirts of Panagia."

The gorgeous man at the wheel had no idea that the thought of spending the rest of the night with him sent her pulse ripping off the charts.

"We can try to get some sleep for what's left of the rest of this night. In the morning, we'll make early rounds of the bike shops."

"We might actually bump into him."

"Or her," he added. "If he's wearing a disguise."

He hadn't forgotten what she'd said. "If not there, maybe at the ferry landing."

"I want to believe that." She was worried sick about Darren of course. Stavros couldn't help but hear the tremor in her voice.

"That makes two of us."

Before too long, he found them a secluded spot. "Do you mind if we don't set up the tent?" His question prompted her to lift her gaze to him, noticing the shadow on his firm jaw. If anything, he was more attractive when he needed a shave.

"No. It's a beautiful night. I've slept out with my father like this hundreds of times. A tent is too confining and we could miss spotting Darren if he were to come this way."

"You're too good to be true. I think I must be dreaming."

"You'll know this is for real if I scream out loud because another ferret the size of the one in the cave creeps onto me."

With a low resonant chuckle he unraveled the bedroll for her to sleep in and made himself a bed on a couple of blankets. They both ate and drank from the contents of the hamper. Then she snuggled into the bedroll and turned on her side toward him.

"Stavros? Thank you for letting me search for Darren with you. I appreciate everything you've done, not only for me, but for him. You're a remarkable man." He was a lot more than that. She needed to turn off her feelings for him. They were spinning out of control.

"Don't give me any credit," he said. "I have just as much at stake here as you. And how long it's taking to find him is convincing me he's more clever than I realized." His hand went to his watch. "I'm setting my alarm so we'll have time to grab some breakfast at one of the cafés first thing in the morning." Andrea watched him pull out his phone. "I'm going to leave a message for the lieutenant about our plans for tomorrow. Then it's lights out."

She turned off her flashlight while she listened. In a minute, he shut the big light off and stretched out on his back with only one blanket pulled over him. He put his hands behind his dark head. "You're a very trusting woman to be out in the forest with me."

"I know the important things," she came back readily. "I did my research and learned that the Konstantinos Corporation enjoys an excellent reputation far and wide for the quality of their products and their fair dealings. The fact that you cared enough to look for Darren on your own time when you didn't have to says a lot about your character."

His compassion and understanding of her loss had really been the things that told her he could be trusted. But she refrained from sharing that with him.

"I'd rather talk about your character, Andrea. No one would expect you to have joined in the search. I'm touched that you would tell me about your harrowing experience waiting to hear news of your fiancé."

She stirred restlessly. "I couldn't just stand by this time. You'd be surprised how many searches I've gone on in the past."

"What do you mean?"

"Living in some of the third-world areas meant helping out in a crisis at a moment's notice. In some ways, it was easier to find someone's lost son or daughter from a remote village than to track down a teen like Darren who wants to be lost in a country as modern and sophisticated as Greece. With money he could be anywhere doing anything. His poor parents must be frantic."

Stavros turned on his side. "Has this happened before on one of the tours?"

"There've been a few serious health issues, but no one ever left in the middle of a tour before. Georgios has been with PanHellenic fifteen years and said he's never had someone disappear on him."

"It's a bizarre situation, one we can't solve tonight."

"You're right. Good night, Stavros." She rolled onto her side away from him.

"Kalinychta, despinis."

His silky voice permeated her body, as if it had found a home. The sensation shocked her before oblivion took over.

The alarm awakened Stavros at six thirty. He hadn't wanted the night to end and was surprised he'd slept. Probably knowing he'd be with her first thing in the morning was the reason he'd fallen off fast. For the first time since he could remember, a woman had come into his life who excited him in inexplicable ways.

Andrea was still asleep, her shiny blond hair splayed around her. He could still feel her wrapped in his arms in the cave. Between that memory and the intensity of those blue eyes fastened on him last night, it was all he could do not to move closer and draw her into his body. But until the boy was found, he needed to focus on matters that could have an adverse impact on everyone involved.

He packed up and started putting everything in the Jeep. When he went back for the hamper, he discovered Andrea had awakened and was rolling up the bedroll.

"Good morning, Stavros." Her smile filled his body with warmth. "How long have you been up?"

"A few minutes."

"Don't tell me if I snore. Some things are better not to know."

She looked so beautiful with her hair in attractive disarray it took all his self-control not to kiss her voluptuous mouth. "You were quiet as a mouse."

"So were you. I think." Despite the seriousness of their situation, she didn't take herself seriously, a trait that appealed to him. They both chuckled.

He took the bedroll from her and put it in the back of the Jeep. She joined him a few minutes later. He noticed she'd brushed her hair and put on a frosted pink lipstick he'd love to taste before he started on her.

Stavros was thunderstruck by his strong physical attraction to her. But right now he needed to concentrate. "Let's go find Darren."

Once they got in the Jeep, he drove back out to the road that led into Panagia. He stopped in front of a cafeteria, where they went in for rolls and coffee. The proprietress recognized him and hurried over to their table.

He questioned her about Darren and showed her his picture from the cell phone. She said she hadn't seen the American teenager in her café, but she'd call the police if he came in.

For the next half hour, they made the rounds of the bike shops. No one had seen the missing teen. When they went back to the Jeep, Andrea turned to him. "I think we should drive to Thassos and watch for him at the marina. He may have stolen someone's bike in order to get there."

"Or maybe he hitched a ride with some local."

"Let's check out all the bars and *tavernas* at the docks. He could be hanging out near the ferry landing stage."

"The police will be searching everywhere, but we'll add our eyes."

For the next two hours, they covered the waterfront, but didn't see anyone who resembled Darren. "Stavros? Let's go on board the ferry that's loading and take a look inside the vehicles. I know the police will have already done that, but maybe they missed something. What do you think?"

He saw the pleading in her eyes. It tugged at him. Neither of them wanted to give up the search, even if the police had already looked here.

"You're reading my mind again."

This was the first ferry of the day leaving for Keramoti. If Darren wanted to get off the island as fast as possible, this would be the one to take.

After parking the Jeep, he paid the fee and they walked on board, following the line of passengers. Since it was a Saturday of full-on summer, crowds of tourists slowed the lines down. He saw two police officers working the line.

Those people with cars had parked them end to end along the sides of the open air hold.

While everyone else went up on the deck to watch

their departure, Stavros and Andrea inspected the interiors of each vehicle. All were empty. There were several small trucks. They eyed each other before he looked in the back of the first one. It was filled with lawn mower equipment.

Andrea moved forward to look inside the back of the next truck parked farther down. Stavros knew she'd found something when she came running toward him. "Quick," she whispered. "There's a tarp covering something. I thought I saw movement and I don't dare lift it off without you."

He grasped her upper arms. Their mouths were only centimeters apart. It was a miracle he restrained himself from kissing her senseless. "You stay here."

Her breathing sounded shallow. "I won't let you do this alone."

Stavros inhaled sharply. "Then stay behind me." After letting her go with reluctance, he walked to the pickup truck in question and took a look for himself. In the next instant, he climbed over the tailgate. Reaching down, he removed the tarp. Sure enough, a body dressed in jeans and tennis shoes was wedged between several packing boxes. A pair of brown eyes stared up at him in shock. His head was resting on his backpack.

"Darren Lewis." Stavros spoke in English, standing over him. "Stay where you are." He pulled out his cell phone and called the police lieutenant.

After a moment the other man answered. "Kyrie Konstantinos? I wish I had better news for you."

"Our worries are over. We've found the missing teenager on board the ferry in Thassos town. He's hiding in the back of a white pickup truck."

"My men said they searched every car."

"This teen has been elusive. Contact the ferry captain and tell him not to leave shore yet. Despinis Linford and I will detain the Lewis boy until you arrive."

"I'll be there in ten minutes."

Stavros helped Andrea up over the tailgate. She thanked him and sat down on one of the packing boxes. By this time, the teen was sitting up, but he didn't try to get away.

"Darren? I'm Andrea Linford from PanHellenic Tours. This is Mr. Konstantinos, the managing director of the Konstantinos Marble Corporation." Not anymore. "We've been looking for you since you disappeared yesterday."

He averted his eyes.

"Your tour director, Georgios, and your teacher, Mrs. Shapiro, have been frantic. Your parents were notified of your disappearance and are on their way here."

The boy went a sickly ashen color. "My mom and dad are coming?"

She nodded. "That's right. The police will take you to them in Thessaloniki."

"I'm eighteen and don't have to see them if I don't want to."

So *that* was what this was about. "Nevertheless, they want to see you," Stavros stated. "Whatever is wrong, nothing can be resolved by running away."

"I hate my father. I never want to see him again."

The pain in his declaration wasn't lost on Stavros or Andrea. "Then you have the legal right to be on your own," he said. "But you're in a foreign country and have broken the law by stowing away in a truck that isn't yours. You have some explaining to do to the police and they'll insist on speaking to you and your parents."

Darren was fighting tears. "I don't want to talk to them."

"I'm afraid you don't have a choice while you're still on Greek soil."

Andrea got on the phone to her boss to tell him the good news. Before long, everyone, including the tour bus group, would know that the crisis had been averted. But the boy's nightmare was just beginning. From past experience, Stavros knew what it was like to be at loggerheads with his own father and had some compassion for Darren, whatever the problem.

"If you're hungry or thirsty, I'll get you something," Andrea volunteered after hanging up. She had a sweetness in her that wasn't lost on Stavros.

"I don't want anything."

"You must have had a bad night. Tell us how you got away from the quarry, Darren."

"I hid underneath someone's truck. When the police walked off, I got inside the back." Andrea and Stavros exchanged glances. "After it stopped at a village, I jumped out and walked down here during the night. While the cars were lined up to board the ferry, I got underneath another truck."

"Even wearing your backpack?" Andrea marveled aloud.

"Yeah. People do it all the time in the movies. When the man parked his truck and left, I climbed in the back and hid under the tarp."

"You were very resourceful." Stavros would give

him that. Six miles wasn't so great a distance. Obviously the boy had handled it without problem.

"Thanks."

Thanks? Even though he was caught? Stavros saw a little of himself in the boy, who was hungry for approbation. Maybe even from his father? He sat down on one of the other packing boxes. "While we're waiting for the lieutenant to come, why don't you tell us why you hate your father so much?"

"He's got my whole life planned out—what he wants me to be, where he wants me to go to college."

Stavros understood Darren better than the teen knew. "What does he want you to be?"

"An attorney like he is and go into politics."

Stavros bowed his head. "And what do you want to be?"

"I don't know yet! One day I'll figure it out."

"Do you have siblings?"

"No. I'm the golden child."

That made the boy's journey much harder. "Now that you're eighteen, you can choose the life you want to live."

Darren looked up at him, imploring him to understand. "Dad just doesn't get it, so I ran away. I wasn't going to stay away a long time."

"You were hoping he'd suffer enough to see the light." Stavros got it. "I have an idea. Go with the police and meet with your parents. Tell them the honest truth. If your father still can't be persuaded, then you'll have to decide whether you can stand to alienate him and go your own way."

Darren nodded. "I can stand it. I don't want to be an attorney."

"But you still love him, right?"

"Yeah."

"Then stick to your guns, but don't shut him out. In time I'm sure things will work out."

"You think?"

"I do."

Tears filled the boy's eyes.

"Here comes the lieutenant. I'll talk to him."

"You will?"

"Of course."

"Thanks for listening." He looked at Andrea. "Thanks for being so nice."

"You're welcome, Darren. Remember how lucky you are to have two parents who care so much. My dad had to raise me because my mom died when I was born. He loved me to death the way I'm sure your parents love you. Try to remain calm when you talk to them. When they see how rational you are, they'll be more receptive."

"I doubt it," he muttered.

Stavros jumped out, then helped Andrea down. "Come on." He turned to Darren, who got to his feet and climbed down the tailgate with his backpack.

While two officers started talking to him, Stavros took the lieutenant aside and told him about the boy's fears. "He's having problems with his father about what he wants to do with his life."

"I had the same problem with my father at that age."

Yup. "I know he's not violent or dangerous. Just unhappy. We've talked and he's promised to go willingly to Thessaloniki and have a talk with his parents. Let me know what happens."

"Of course. Congratulations on finding him so quickly. This is a great relief for everyone."

"He might not have been caught without the help of Despinis Linford."

The lieutenant turned to shake her hand before following his officers, who escorted Darren off the ferry to the police van. The teen waved to them. They waved back.

Stavros looked at Andrea and glimpsed tears in her fabulous blue eyes. She was equally anxious for Darren to reconcile with his father. "Let's go home, Andrea."

They left the ferry and hurried to the Jeep. When they got inside, she buried her face in her hands. It took all his control not to pull her into his arms. "I'm so thankful we found him."

He turned on the engine and drove out of the parking area. "You're not alone."

She finally lifted her head. "Because of the problems you've had with your father, you were wonderful with him. It touched my heart. You gave him hope and the direction he needed. I'm in awe of the way you handled a very difficult situation."

Moved by her words, he glanced at her. "The lieutenant will fill me in after they release him to his parents. In the meantime, all we can do is hope this means the beginning of some kind of reconciliation, but it's not our problem."

She wiped her eyes. "No. Thank heaven he's no longer missing. That's because of you. I couldn't have done the search for him I wanted without your help."

Satisfied he could concentrate on her from now on, he lounged back in the seat. "We worked well together. After our fine piece of detective work, we deserve the best lunch I can make for us after we reach the house."

"Only if you let me help."

"Do you like to cook?"

"If I have the time."

He liked the sound of that since he had plans for them for the rest of the weekend. When they reached the villa, he walked her to the guest room. "I'm sure you'd prefer a shower before we eat. I need one myself and a shave. There's a robe and toiletries in the en suite bathroom for the use of guests. Bring your clothes to the kitchen and we'll get them washed while we eat."

She looked away, but he caught the flush on her cheeks. "I couldn't impose on you."

Stavros had been waiting for that response. "I'm afraid you don't have any say in the matter. We camped out in the forest all night. You helped a teacher and tour guide hold on to their jobs and saved your company and mine from notoriety we don't need. When you get to know me better, you'll find out I'm prepared to indulge you endlessly."

Before she had time to argue, he walked away from her.

CHAPTER THREE

ANDREA HUNG ON to the handle after she'd shut the door to the bedroom. Had he said *endlessly*?

She knew he was grateful that both their companies had been spared making headlines in the media. But his comment had indicated something more personal. For a man like Stavros Konstantinos to be interested in a foreigner working for a tour company when he could have any woman he wanted didn't make sense.

After removing her clothes, she went into the bathroom and stood under the shower, but she couldn't get him off her mind. While they'd been talking last night, she'd inferred he was allergic to marriage, but he'd admitted to having girlfriends. Naturally he did. With his kind of potent male charisma, what woman in her right mind would resist him?

Her thoughts flicked to Ferrante, who had attracted her for other reasons, particularly his happy nature. You couldn't compare him to Stavros, who was more brooding. They were in different leagues. Andrea couldn't think of another man who measured up to the dynamic member of the Konstantinos family. Though she knew he was powerful when necessary, she admired the kind way he'd handled Darren when he'd found him.

Intuition told her he was the real force behind the corporation's success. He was a man who lit his own fires in spite of his father's heavy hand. Who wouldn't admire him for the courage of his beliefs? Last night he'd told her they'd find Darren and she'd believed him.

In the light of day she realized it was amazing she'd trusted him enough to spend the night alone with him. He'd had that effect on her. Such a complete effect, in fact, she was taking a shower in his villa before joining him for lunch.

Andrea shut off the water and stepped out on the bath mat surrounded by a floor of gleaming white Thassos marble. A white toweling robe hung on a hook on the back of the door, but she stopped short of walking around his home in it.

Just remembering that moment on the ferry when he'd grasped her arms to keep her from danger made her breath catch. His lips had come too close to hers. Here they'd been looking for Darren, yet she'd wanted him to kiss her.

You need to go home, Andrea.

When she got back to her apartment she would wash her clothes.

After reaching for a towel to dry off, she brushed her teeth and then went back to the bedroom to put on her blouse and skirt. A thorough brushing of her hair, a coat of lipstick, and she was ready to face her host for a meal before she left for Thessaloniki.

Her stomach growled as she walked on stunning stone-and-marble floors on her way to the kitchen.

Everywhere she looked she saw the ancient blue-and-white Greek pattern, whether it was on the tufted cushion of a couch or a vase of flowers. During her rare shopping jaunts, she'd learned its geometric elegance was thought to resemble the waves of the sea and shapes of labyrinths, a symbol for infinity.

When she reached the kitchen, she found Stavros putting a salad together and hoped he hadn't heard her hunger pains. While they'd been apart, he'd showered and shaved. Andrea could smell the soap he'd used. It was impossible not to stare at the way the white collared polo and khaki trousers fit his incredible physique.

His gaze played over her, but he made no comment that she wasn't wearing the robe. "Except for a dip in the ocean, there's nothing as refreshing as a shower. I've got lunch ready and thought we'd eat out on the patio."

"What can I do to help?"

His black brows lifted. "Not a thing except to join me."

"Do you know I'm getting more indebted to you by the minute?"

"What if I told you I like the odds?"

Avoiding those penetrating gray eyes, she said, "Well, as you can see, I'm not complaining."

She followed him through an alcove to the patio with a lattice covering and was greeted with a breathtaking view of the Aegean. They sat down to a glass-topped round table. He'd provided iced tea and rolls, along with a salad of olives, feta cheese, tomatoes and chunks of succulent chicken.

They both ate with a healthy appetite. "This is delicious."

"Again, I can't take the credit."

Andrea put down her fork. "You're talking about your housekeeper."

He nodded. "Raisa."

"Does she live with you?"

"No. She and her husband live in Panagia. She comes twice a week to clean the house and keep my fridge stocked."

"You're an interesting man, Stavros. Every time I want to talk about you, you somehow change the subject, but this time it won't work. There *is* something for which you can take full credit."

His eyes swerved to hers. "What's that?"

"When you discovered Darren lying there between the boxes, you could have come down hard on him with every right, yet the opposite happened. Maybe if his own father treated him the gentle, reasonable way you did, the two of them wouldn't have a problem. One day, you're going to make a terrific father."

Something seemed to flicker in those pewter depths. "I was just about to pay you a similar compliment. Instead of berating him, you asked if he needed food or water. Under the circumstances, your compassion was refreshing."

"Surely not. Anyone could see he was just a teenager, even if he'd just turned eighteen. You could tell he was frightened."

"Not everyone would have responded the way you did."

Her mouth curved into an impish smile. "Then that must make both of us exceptional human beings."

Except for his smiling eyes, she didn't know how Stavros would have reacted because a female voice had called out from the interior of the villa. In the next instant, he got to his feet in time for an attractive woman with silver in her cap of black hair to appear at the patio entrance. She looked maybe early sixties and was stylishly dressed in a summer suit.

"*Mama*—I didn't hear the helicopter." He walked over and gave her a kiss on both cheeks. "Why didn't you call to tell me you were coming?"

"I didn't want you to know, *o gios mou*. When I heard the news yesterday that you've left the company, my heart failed me."

Andrea was stunned. Stavros had left the Konstantinos Corporation?

"I've been planning it for a long time. You know that."

"I never believed it would really happen." She shook her head. "When I couldn't find you at your condo, I decided to pay an unannounced visit to the island to find out what has possessed you to do this. You've caused an explosion in the family that has shaken it to the very foundation."

"It'll run smoothly without me."

That was Stavros's modesty talking. Andrea was still trying to comprehend it.

"Why have you done this?" his mother cried. "I don't understand. Neither does your father. He's livid that you chose the board meeting to make an announcement that has hurt him to the core."

"He'll live."

At his response, Andrea's hand gripped her glass tighter.

"How can you be so cold?"

"I've always gone my own way. This is nothing new."

"When you talk like this, I can't believe you're our son. What has happ—?" His mother suddenly stopped midsentence because she'd just spotted Andrea seated at the table. Her cool brown gaze took swift inventory as she moved toward her. "But I'm interrupting and can see you have a guest. No wonder you didn't hear the helicopter arriving."

"I'd like you to meet Despinis Linford."

Andrea stood up and shook the older woman's hand. She admired Stavros's aplomb in handling what had turned into a painful confrontation. A lesser man wouldn't be able to brush his mother's concerns aside with such diplomacy. But it was obvious Stavros had the strength to swim against the tide when necessary.

She hadn't truly understood some of the dynamics of his family until this moment. More than ever, she knew the Konstantinos Corporation would suffer with him gone. But she sensed there was something that went even deeper for his mother to show up like this.

"It's a pleasure to meet you, Kyria Konstantinos."

"Would you like some iced tea, Mama?"

"Please." She sat down on one of the chairs near the railing. He poured a glass and walked it over to her. His mother took a sip before she regarded Andrea. "I had no idea my son wasn't alone." She looked at him. "Are you going to enlighten me?"

Stavros lounged against the railing, the urbane host. "Andrea works at the headquarters of PanHellenic Tours in Thessaloniki. An incident at the quarry developed yesterday, and she came to investigate." Without hesitation he explained what had happened, but left out certain details his mother didn't need to know "The teen was found today and returned to his parents. We've been having a celebratory lunch."

She frowned. "Maybe now you'll understand why allowing tour groups at the quarry isn't a good idea. You should have listened to your father."

His mouth tightened into a white line. "Careful, Mama, or you'll hurt Andrea's feelings. She's the one who approached our corporation in order to add it to the student itineraries. Like me, she's anxious to increase the public's education concerning one of Greece's greatest resources. I'm glad my grandfather thought it would be beneficial and backed me before he passed away."

Andrea was subjected to another taste of his mother's disapproving scrutiny. "Where are you from?"

"I was born in Denver, Colorado, but I've lived in many places around the world with my father."

"She's fluent in many languages besides English and Greek," Stavros interjected. "It might interest you to know she received her degree from Aristotle University."

Needing to stop the inquisition in the most polite way she knew how, Andrea got up from the table. "Stavros fixed our lunch, Kyria Konstantinos, so the least I can do is clear up. Since you came to talk with your son, I'll give you some privacy and do the dishes before I leave. Please excuse me."

Whatever his reaction, Andrea avoided looking at him. After gathering up their plates and glasses, she headed for the kitchen. When she went back to get the salad bowl, she discovered the two of them had disappeared, which was a relief.

Once she'd restored the kitchen to order, she reached for her purse and went out to the patio to wait for him. The view was so heavenly, it almost didn't seem real. A few minutes later, he made an appearance alone and stood in front of her with his hands on his hips in a forbidding male stance. His fierce expression was so different from that of the relaxed host who'd made their lunch earlier. She could hardly believe she was looking at the same man.

"I apologize for my mother, Andrea."

She shook her head. "Why? Among other things, I now know where you get your good looks."

"Because she walked in on me when she knew better." Andrea decided he hadn't even heard the compliment she'd paid him.

"She's your mom, and she was obviously so upset about the news she'd heard and was afraid you would remain unreachable."

"That's no excuse for rude behavior. To be honest, she has never burst in on me before in my own home." Andrea believed him. "She's normally quite gracious. I can promise you that my resignation from the company had little to do with her springing herself on me the way she did."

Andrea didn't know the exact reason for his mother's reaction, but the sight of a strange woman with her son had set her off even more. There was more to that story, as he'd said, but it was none of her business.

"You don't owe me any explanation, Stavros. I need to get the car back to Thassos and catch the next ferry, but I waited so I could thank you for everything."

His black brows furrowed. "Your boss won't be expecting you before Monday. Why are you in such a rush?"

Her heart pounded too hard in her chest. "I have work waiting at the office that must be done before next week."

He cocked his handsome head. "I think you're trying to get away from me."

The best way to handle this was to agree with him. She smiled. "I admit it. But if you remember, I asked if you would let me come with you to look for Darren. Since the crisis is over, it's time for me to get back to Thessaloniki."

After a short silence, "What if I want you to stay?" His husky tone played havoc with her senses.

She took a fortifying breath. "Forgive me for being blunt, but I can't afford to stay." *I'm far too attracted to you.*

How could she feel this strongly about him when Ferrante hadn't died that long ago? She didn't want to know the pain of loving someone again and was shocked at the strength of her feelings for him already. A prominent man like Stavros Konstantinos could have his pick of any woman, but he could never be serious about her. It wasn't worth risking her heart to stay around any longer, especially when she'd be leaving the country with her father in the not-too-distant future.

"Thank you again for letting me play detective with you. I won't forget your generosity."

Andrea walked past him and out the rear door of

the house to her car. It was the longest walk of her life. Getting away from him now meant she'd escaped before it was too late. To remain here another minute would be putting herself in emotional jeopardy.

She'd had enough time to think about his mother's shock at finding her son with Andrea. Stavros had admitted this had nothing to do with his recent business decision, but it was all too much of a mystery for Andrea. She pressed on the gas as she made her way down the mountain.

As Andrea was finding out, Stavros was more complicated than she'd first realized. Not so Ferrante, who'd been open with her from the start. No mystery, no secrets. He'd asked Andrea to marry him. He'd wanted a life with her. Marriage, children. The whole thing. Why that fierce mountain blizzard had to come along and destroy their dream, she didn't know.

The first set of tears she'd shed for him in a long time made her vision blurry. She needed to slow down or she'd get in an accident. Maybe it would be years before an uncomplicated man like Ferrante came along again. Maybe never.

Forget Stavros Konstantinos!

"Andrea? I know it's time for you to go home, but would you step into my office for a minute, please?"

She couldn't say no to Sakis, but it *was* Friday night. Her single friend Dorcas worked in the accounts department for the tour company on the next floor up. Maybe she'd want to get some dinner and go to a film later with Andrea. After she talked to Sakis, she'd give her a call.

"I'll be right there."

The mock-up for the latest itinerary just needed a few finishing touches, but it could wait until Monday. She closed the file, backed it up on the computer and reached for her purse in the bottom drawer of her desk. A little lipstick and a quick brush of her hair would have to do to make herself presentable.

Andrea said good-night to a couple of coworkers as she walked past their desks to reach Sakis's office. The door was closed, so she knocked.

"Come in!"

Sakis, in shirtsleeves, reminded Andrea of an overweight newspaper editor who smoked, drank tons of coffee and talked with ten situations going on at the same time. He loved to tell crass jokes to provoke a reaction. But for once she didn't even notice him because there was another man in the office, seated across from his desk. A striking, dark-haired male dressed in a gray business suit and tie. The sight of him robbed her of breath.

Stavros.

No, no, no. A week had gone by since she'd left his villa. It wasn't enough time...

He got to his feet, making her more aware of his virility than ever. Stavros didn't have to try to knock a woman dead. It just happened automatically in his presence.

"Andrea," he murmured in that deep voice. "How are you?"

How am I? She was reeling. "Fine, thank you. And you?"

"I wasn't fine until now."

Warmth spread up her neck and face.

"Sit down, my dear." Sakis indicated the chair

next to Stavros, unaware of her shock. "I've wanted to speak to both of you since the incident with the Lewis boy. But Kyrie Konstantinos couldn't break away from business matters until now."

Sakis had phoned Stavros?

"Words can't express my gratitude to both of you for finding the teen in such a short period of time. An international incident was avoided, sparing both our companies adverse publicity and possible litigation."

Andrea sat forward. "We're all happy about that. Do you have any news of how he is now?"

"I understand he's back in Connecticut with his parents."

"He told us he was upset with his father. That's why he tried to run away."

Sakis spread his hands apart. "It happens. My son has threatened to kill me several times." But he laughed when he said it. In that moment, Stavros's eyes sent her a silent message, as if to say the two of them knew the teen's situation hadn't been a laughing matter.

Her boss sat back in his swivel chair. "Kyrie Konstantinos? The police lieutenant told me you influenced him not to bring charges against the teen." Andrea hadn't known that. "Such a gesture on your part is amazing."

"Nonsense. Except to worry everyone, the teen did no harm."

"Not everyone is as forgiving as you."

As Andrea had already come to find out, Stavros was no ordinary man.

"I've brought you two together to get your opinion about continuing the tours to the quarry. Another incident like this one might not turn out so well next time." He eyed Stavros. "Would you prefer we cancel future tours? It's up to you."

"I'm afraid it won't be up to me any longer," Stavros stated. "I've resigned from the Konstantinos Marble Corporation. I suggest you phone the company immediately and ask for Dimitri."

Sakis's eyes rounded. "You resigned?"

"That's right. Life is full of surprises and difficulties. Hopefully the new CEO won't stop these tours because of one troubled teenager."

Sakis looked genuinely upset. "We're very sorry to hear this, aren't we, Andrea?"

"Yes," she said, aware of Stavros's gaze. "To see the resources of the earth up close gives you a new reverence for the whole plan of creation. Mounds and mounds of marble here from the beginning of time for men to use."

"I believe you're wasted in this office," Sakis said. "You should be a publicist out selling Greece to the world."

"You're full of it," she teased, but was pleased by the rare compliment, especially in front of Stavros.

He extinguished the last of his cigarette. "All right. I'll make the call. In light of this information, thank you for coming in person, Kyrie Konstantinos. Nothing would have been possible without your generosity." Stavros *was* a generous man. Andrea had firsthand knowledge. "We're honored that you would allow our tours to come on your property."

"It has been my pleasure."

Sakis stood and shook his hand. "The arrangement worked well for everyone."

"Perhaps it will still work. Good luck."

But Stavros's father hadn't approved, not according to his mother. With Andrea's heart racing now that this meeting was over, she got to her feet. It was imperative she get away from Stavros. "Have a good weekend, Sakis."

"You too. See you on Monday."

"I'll be here."

She left the office first, hoping to lose Stavros by going down in the elevator. But when she found she had to wait for it, she opted for the stairs.

Stavros caught up to her at the landing, not the least winded. "Where's the fire, *despinis*?"

Andrea darted him a glance. "I have a bus to catch." She knew she was behaving like an idiot, but she was afraid of her feelings for him.

"You don't own a car?"

"I don't need one in town. When Dad comes home, I use his." She kept going until she came out into the foyer.

"I'll drive you home."

"I appreciate the offer, but it isn't necessary."

"I'm afraid it's of vital importance to me."

Something in his tone made her realize he wasn't toying with her. She stopped walking and looked at him. "That sounded serious."

"At last I've gotten through to you. Do you have plans for this evening?"

Andrea could lie, but was resigned that he would see through it. "No."

"You do now. The limo is waiting out in front. I'll run you home so you can change into something comfortable and pack an overnight bag. Bring a bathing suit. I want to spend the weekend with you. Surely that couldn't come as a surprise—or am I wrong and you have no interest in me?"

That meant two nights alone with him. Her body started to tremble. "I think you're an exceptional man."

He studied her through veiled eyes. "Yet you don't trust me?"

"That's not the point." *I'm the one I don't trust.*

"Then there's no problem, is there?"

She lifted her head. "If Sakis hadn't asked you to come to his office, this wouldn't be happening."

"Contrary to what you believe, I would have gotten hold of you earlier in the week. But certain business matters prevented me from doing what I wanted to do. I purposely arranged this meeting with your boss at the end of your work week so we could be together."

Oh, Stavros, she moaned inwardly. "I'm not sure this is a good idea."

"My mother's interruption upset you, but she won't do it again."

"This doesn't have anything to do with your mother. I'm just not ready to get involved with another man."

"You're still mourning Ferrante, aren't you?"

"Yes. I may not be actively grieving for him, but I have a full plate with my work and can't handle anything else."

"Up until today you've been honest with me. Why can't you be truthful now?"

"Because I don't want to get hurt again!" she blurted in exasperation.

"I don't plan to hurt you," he said in that velvety voice she couldn't ignore.

"Mother died. Ferrante died."

"I don't plan on doing that anytime soon," came the wry reply. "What happened to the girl who takes risks traveling around to third-world countries and was willing to spend the night in a forest with a near stranger? Where did that girl go?"

"You know what I meant," she murmured.

"No. I don't. Do you think I'm some kind of womanizer?"

Andrea couldn't look at him. "I have no way of knowing, do I?"

"Did you give Ferrante this much trouble when he showed interest in you?"

"Let's not bring him into this." To care about Stavros meant going through more heartache again. After Ferrante, she couldn't handle it.

"Why not? Afraid to give me an answer?"

"No."

"He was a mountain-climbing guide and would have been around beautiful women all the time. Did you accuse him of using them?"

"Of course not."

"So how come you're having trust issues with me when you don't really know me yet? I thought you liked me a little."

"You know I do," she whispered fiercely.

"Then spend the weekend with me. If you discover I'm not worth knowing, then so be it."

Andrea couldn't find fault with his logic. It was her heart she was worried about. He might decide she wasn't worth knowing.

"We're wasting time. What's your address?"

He'd broken her down so fast she couldn't think. When she answered him, he cupped her elbow and walked her out to the limo. "Let's hurry. We'll take the helicopter from the airport and eat dinner on Thassos."

That meant they were going back to his fabulous villa. Andrea hadn't thought to ever see him again, let alone stay in that heavenly place. She closed her eyes, full of questions and incredulous this was happening.

She still had time to tell him no, but her self-control had deserted her. Throughout the week she'd done everything possible to put him out of her mind. But her heart had leaped the second she'd seen him sitting in Sakis's office. It was still leaping. Andrea was terrified it might always remain in that state.

CHAPTER FOUR

STAVROS SAT IN the copilot's seat, but looked over his shoulder at Andrea, who, from her seat behind the pilot, was devouring the lush scenery of Thassos Island. This was the first time he'd seen her wearing jeans. An ivory linen jersey top with sleeves pushed up to the elbow covered her womanly figure. Between that and her honey-blond coloring, he had trouble not devouring her.

A trip like this would never be wasted on her because she was a female of exceptional intelligence and she had an interest in everything. "Is this the first time you've seen Thassos from the air?"

Andrea nodded. "I'm glad it's not too dark yet. The green of it is almost unreal."

His gaze locked with her azure-blue eyes. "It has different looks, but twilight is the most beautiful time to see it."

"Were you born on the island?"

"No. Thessaloniki. All my family lives there, but I fell in love with Thassos the first time my father brought me to one of the quarries. When I climbed to the top of Mount Ypsarion for the first time, I knew

I wanted to live here and planned exactly where I would build my house one day."

"You're very fortunate to have realized your dream. Not all of us can do that."

"It was only one of them, Andrea. Since then I've had more. What was yours?"

"That's easy to answer. When I was little, I used to play dolls with my friend and pretend my mommy was alive. I would dream that she came back to life and lived with me and Daddy. By the age of six, I realized that dream would never be realized in this life. I haven't dreamed since."

The pathos of the moment produced a lump in his throat. "Do you have a picture of her with you?"

She blinked. "A couple."

"When we reach the house, I'd like to see them. Are you hungry?"

"Starving."

"My housekeeper has our dinner waiting for us."

"Oh, good. I'm thankful we don't have to cook anything. I don't think I could wait that long."

He laughed. Her honesty was one of the many traits he admired about her. "We'll be at the villa within a few minutes."

His gaze traveled to her practical duffel bag stowed on the other seat. No designer luggage for her. She'd traipsed around the world with her father and had discovered that less was always better than more.

The pilot dipped them down to the landing pad. It had been built on the west side of the villa with steps leading up and around the foliage to the front entrance. Stavros had planned it that way so it would be out of sight.

When he was in the house, he could usually hear the rotors. But last week he'd been so enthralled with Andrea, he hadn't realized his mother had arrived in his father's helicopter until she'd walked out on the patio.

So much had happened in a week. Through Leon, he'd found out their older cousin Dimitri had been promoted to CEO. Dimitri had wanted to be in charge for a long time. As for the state of affairs between Stavros and his parents, they couldn't be worse. There'd been only one brief phone call from his mother since she'd left the villa.

He'd known how disappointed she was that he'd stopped seeing Tina, but he'd never dreamed she'd show rudeness in front of Andrea. Tonight he wanted to make it up to Andrea and planned to concentrate on the two of them.

Once they were on the ground, he thanked the pilot and helped Andrea down from the helicopter. After grabbing her duffel bag, he climbed out and ushered her up the steps to the front door of the house. To his surprise, Raisa opened it before he could use his remote. He'd thought she would have gone home by now.

"Kyrie..." she said in a hushed voice. "You have a visitor. Despinis Nasso arrived an hour ago by car and insisted on staying until you returned. I showed her into the living room."

He couldn't believe this had happened right after the conversation with Andrea about other women. Stavros decided he *was* cursed and ground his teeth.

Tina must have parked around the back. With the exception of Andrea, he'd never brought another woman to his house. The only way Tina could have found out where to come was through his mother.

When she had finally called earlier that day, his mother had begged him to come to dinner at the house with her and his father. No doubt she'd been contriving a small party that included Tina. He'd told her he would have to miss it because he had important business back on Thassos.

For Tina to show up here meant his family had declared war on him and wouldn't hesitate to use Tina to achieve their objective.

"Thank you, Raisa."

He turned to Andrea. "I apologize for another unexpected interruption. Please make yourself at home in the guest bedroom while I deal with this. I'll only be a minute."

But the second the words left his mouth, Tina appeared in the front hallway. She looked fashionably turned out in a pale pink suit that highlighted her long black hair. "I'm sorry, Stavros. I heard the helicopter, but I had no idea you'd be coming home with company. You didn't answer my phone calls or my texts. I need to talk to you privately."

Even if she had his mother's permission, her effrontery appalled him. "I'm afraid that's not possible. We said our goodbyes over three months ago. You weren't invited here. Please have the courtesy to leave."

With a sangfroid that chilled him, her gaze swerved to Andrea and the duffel bag. "You must be the American woman who works for PanHellenic Tours. Stavros forgot to introduce us. I'm Tina Lasso."

Ice filled his veins. He opened the door for her. "Goodbye, Tina."

She walked toward him. "I've just come from your parents and thought you'd want to know I'm pregnant with your child."

The oldest lie in the world. Tina had sunk to an all-time low.

"I never slept with you, Tina." The words came out like a quiet hiss. "If you *are* pregnant, it isn't mine."

"Oh, darling," she said after stepping outside. " Do you really expect Despinis Linford to believe that?"

"I have no expectations, Tina, only sadness that you've let our parents' wishes rule your life. Once you start thinking for yourself, you'll never have to be desperate again."

Spots of red filled her cheeks. "How dare you—"

He closed the door in her face, attempting to gain control of his anger. Not so much at her. She was a puppet. This kind of behavior happened to the inse-cure offspring of parents who didn't know what life was all about, yet were determined to impose their will at any cost.

Out of the stillness came a voice. "If she *is* preg-nant with your baby, then you should run after her. Don't let my being here stop you."

Stavros wheeled around. "It couldn't be my baby."

Andrea's solemn eyes stared straight into his. "The same thing happened to Dad one time in Venezuela after he'd decided not to see this one woman anymore. As it turned out, she wasn't pregnant, but she'd hoped he would believe the lie and marry her. Is this Tina that kind of woman? Or could she be telling the truth?"

He sucked in his breath. "Tina comes from a good family and is the woman my parents have expected me to marry. We spent some time together, but I couldn't love her. Once again, I've disappointed them by preferring to choose my own wife when the time comes.

"I haven't seen her for over three months. She could be pregnant, but not with my baby. We were never intimate. Naturally you have no way of knowing if I'm telling the truth or not. If you want to leave now, I'll ask the pilot to fly you back to Thessaloniki."

Her answer was a long time in coming. "My father never lied to me, so I had no reason not to believe him. So far, I don't believe you've lied to me about anything either. Under the circumstances, I prefer to reserve judgment. On that note, do you think we can eat now?"

"Andrea—"

Without conscious thought he crushed her against his chest. Holding her was all he'd been able to think about since the moment they'd met. Losing track of time, he rocked her in his arms while he clung to her. As he started kissing her hair and cheek, her stomach rumbled. He not only heard it, he felt it, and they both broke into laughter.

"You probably think *I've* got a baby inside *me*."

Drowning in her smile, he was on the verge of covering her mouth with his own when he heard, *"Kyrie?"*

His housekeeper's voice had sounded on cue.

"Your dinner is on the table in the dining room. I'm leaving now."

Andrea eased herself away.

"Thank you, Raisa." He grasped Andrea's hand and drew her toward the dining room off the other end of the kitchen. For the time being, she was willing to trust him. It was a gift beyond price. He felt as if he'd been let out of a dark prison where he'd been chained for years and years and had suddenly emerged into blinding sunlight that filled his whole being.

His housekeeper had prepared oven-baked lamb and crab salad. For dessert, she'd fixed his favorite grape must pudding. Between him and Andrea they made short work of it.

When they'd finished, she let out a deep sigh of contentment. "That has to be the best meal I've ever eaten. How did you find her? She's worth her weight in gold."

"Her husband worked at the quarry until retirement. He became ill last year and I often dropped by to visit him."

"What a kind thing to do."

"I had an agenda. Raisa always forced food on me. One day, I told her I'd pay a king's ransom if she'd be my cook. They needed the money, so she took me up on it."

"Is he still sick?"

"He gets bouts of pneumonia, but so far he's managing."

While he sat there drinking his coffee, she got up to clear the table and clean up the kitchen. She'd probably been in the habit of waiting on her father. As Stavros was discovering, old habits died hard.

"Andrea? Come back in the dining room and bring your purse so I can see those pictures of your family."

"I only have three in my wallet."

She returned and pulled them out so he could picture her parents. One of the photos showed her mother pregnant. She'd been a lovely blonde woman. "You strongly resemble her."

"Dad says the same thing."

Andrea's lean, chemical engineer father had rugged features with light brown hair and blue eyes. "To a Greek like me, your parents represent the handsome American couple."

She smiled and sat down to drink the rest of her coffee. "Why do we look American?"

"I don't know. Your mannerisms maybe. The way you hold yourself. I really can't explain it."

"You Greeks give off your own vibes too. At first, Sakis didn't want to hire me because it would give a non-Greek a job." She put the photos away.

"But he was already smitten," Stavros murmured, unable to prevent himself from eating her up with his eyes. "I saw it at his office. Combined with your résumé, he was hooked. That was a lucky day for him and my family's corporation, even if my grandfather was the only one who had vision."

A gentle laugh escaped. "Do you miss him?"

"Very much. Just once, he admitted that my father was a harsh taskmaster. He said it surprised him. That was my grandfather's way of telling me he approved of me."

Her eyes misted over. "How difficult for you. I'm sorry."

"Don't be. I've grown a second skin. I'd rather talk about you. Are you planning to stay with PanHellenic Tours as a career?"

"Oh, no. Only until my father leaves for his new assignment in Indonesia."

Stavros felt as though he'd just been punched in the gut. That was one answer he hadn't expected. "How soon will he be leaving Greece?"

"Mid-October."

Less than two months?

His stomach muscles tightened in reaction. "That country has seen a lot of turmoil."

"Not where Dad and I will be living."

Stavros stifled a groan. "Does your boss know yet?"

"Yes. Why do you ask?"

"The way he talked with you today, I got the feeling he won't want to let you go."

"We've had a good relationship, but he always knew I'd leave when my father had to relocate."

He rubbed the back of his neck. "Is that what you want to do?"

A haunted look crossed over her classic features. "Dad and I have never been separated. If Ferrante hadn't died, we were going to live with my father wherever his work took him. Ferrante planned to give up his job. He was a linguist and would have found work with me so we could be together. The climb up Mont Blanc was going to be his last. As it turned out, it was his final climb." Her voice shook.

Stavros reached out to squeeze her hand before releasing it. "How old was he?"

"Twenty-seven."

Ferrante had been young and so much in love with Andrea, he was willing to give up his interests to be with her. He didn't know any man willing to do that. But to live with her father? Why? That question was on the tip of his tongue, but he didn't feel now was the time to broach the subject.

Her father couldn't be an invalid—otherwise he wouldn't be working at a mine site. Stavros didn't understand. "What about his family?"

"We planned to fly to Ticino for vacations to be with his parents." Her soulful eyes searched his. "What's wrong, Stavros?"

What *wasn't*!

"Nothing important." This new information had knocked him sideways. "Do you know your eyelids are drooping? It's getting late and I must confess I'm tired too. Why don't we put off more talk until tomorrow?" He needed time to think.

"You're a master at hiding your feelings, but I happen to know the incident in the foyer a little while ago has upset you. If you want to talk about it, I'm a good listener."

Stavros had already forgotten about it, but it was just as well she didn't know what was really bothering him. "I've already learned that about you and will take you up on your offer in the morning."

"Then I'll say good-night."

She shot out of the chair with her purse and disappeared from the dining room before he realized her intentions. He could have called her to come back, but then he'd have to admit he couldn't comprehend his life without her in it. *That* was what was bothering him.

He'd never wanted a woman so much in his life. But if he told her this soon, she'd never believe him. Stavros hardly believed it himself. What had it been? Only a week since they'd met each other? It was asking too much of her when she'd just been witness to Tina's lie, a lie Stavros couldn't rule out definitively without proof.

On top of that nightmare was the news she'd be leaving with her father in October. Stavros was staggered by tonight's events. He might as well have been smashed by one of those enormous marble slabs being loaded on one of the flatbed trucks. Heaven knew there'd be no sleep for him tonight. As for all the other nights to come, it didn't bear thinking about.

After Andrea reached the guest bedroom, she shut the door and rummaged for the cell phone in her purse. Maybe her dad was already asleep, but she needed to hear his voice. Her call went through to his voice mail. She left a message for him to call her back when he could.

Once she'd taken a quick shower and brushed her teeth, she climbed into bed with a bestselling Jean Sasson novel. She needed to keep her mind occupied so she wouldn't think about a troubled Stavros somewhere in the villa. If Tina had lied, then he had to be enraged.

When he'd locked Andrea in his arms a little while ago, it had felt so right she'd never wanted to leave them. Her heart had steamed into his. He was beyond wonderful. No man could compare to him.

Andrea couldn't imagine what it was like for Stavros to live with that kind of pressure to marry a woman his family had picked out for him. How sad his grandfather wasn't still alive.

But what if Stavros had lied to Andrea...?

She barely knew him, yet until Tina had appeared, Andrea had felt she knew all the important things about the core of him. In her heart, she didn't believe he would lie to her. *Because you don't want to?*

Her thoughts went back to Tina Nasso. Maybe she *was* pregnant, just not with Stavros's baby. If that was true, then to confront him with Andrea standing there was a desperate act. Wretched and unconscionable, if Stavros wasn't the father. What a nightmare for Stavros, who, through it all, had shown remarkable restraint.

She'd never known pressure from her father. With him for a role model, she knew the kind of man she wanted to marry. One who had her dad's goodness and gentleness. When she'd told her father she loved Ferrante and planned to get married, he'd been totally accepting because he'd liked him from the beginning.

Maybe it was different between fathers and sons. Stavros's mother had come right out, in front of Andrea, about her husband's disapproval of the quarry tours Stavros had sanctioned. Those outspoken words—meant to chastise Stavros—had hurt Andrea for him.

Her thoughts jumped to Sakis, who had admitted

to problems with his son. Though he'd made light of it, Andrea suspected his son probably wouldn't laugh.

She decided she was the luckiest daughter in the world to have such a fantastic father. After showing Stavros her pictures, she was feeling exceptionally emotional. When the phone rang and she saw the caller ID, she picked up and blurted, "Dad? Do you have any idea how much I love you?"

He laughed for a long time. "I love you too, honey. What has brought all this on?"

"Things. Life." Her voice wobbled. "Every day I appreciate you more and more. A lot has happened since we last talked."

"For me too. If you hadn't phoned, *I* would have. You need to give your boss notice in the morning."

How strange he would mention her boss when Stavros had just questioned her about her job earlier. Alert to a serious tone in his voice, she sat up in bed. "What's wrong?"

"Nothing to do with me personally, honey. It looks like there's too much political unrest at the mine in Papua. Remember my telling you about the Free Papua Movement?"

"Vaguely."

"They've turned into a revolutionary organization whose purpose is to overthrow the government in Papua and West Papua. It has been blamed for a lot of attacks happening near the mine."

Stavros had mentioned the turmoil there. The Konstantinos Corporation did business all over the world. That was why he knew everything.

"My company doesn't want me taking any chances, so I won't be going there after all."

That meant they wouldn't be leaving Greece for a long time! *Thank you, thank you,* her heart whispered.

"The good news is, they're sending me to Brazil for a short-term assignment. I have to be there in ten days. At this point, I'm finishing up my work here as fast as I can."

Andrea reeled. Wait a minute—in ten days she'd never see Stavros again? How was she going to handle that?

"Think you can be ready by then?"

She slid out of bed, too upset by his news to lie there. "O-of course I can." Her voice faltered. "But the lease on the apartment isn't up until the middle of October. We'll have to pay for the time we won't be living in it."

"No problem. I'll take care of it. Honey, this short-term assignment in Brazil will be my last one. While we're there, you don't need to get a job. It might be fun for you to work on the language and add Portuguese to your long list."

Andrea held the phone tighter. She'd been listening, but one comment stood out. "What do you mean your last one?"

"I'm finally tired of moving around. I miss Denver, and the main office wants me there. By Thanksgiving we'll be home for good."

Home? For good? She'd never heard him sound so happy. His excitement rang in her ears.

"We'll buy a house and I'll get all the furniture and possessions out of storage."

She had to sink down on the side of the bed or she would have fainted on the spot. Her father sounded so ecstatic about his future plans, she didn't want to say anything to change that excitement. Denver was a long way away from Thassos Island. She couldn't believe it, but her father sounded homesick.

"Now tell me what's been going on with you, honey."

Tears trickled down her cheeks. "Nothing as important as your news. I'll fill you in later. Get a good sleep. I'll call you soon. Love you, Dad." She clicked off.

For his whole life, he'd taken perfect care of her. He'd taken her everywhere with him so they'd never be apart. Now he wanted to go home and assumed she'd be going home with him.

Up until a week ago, she would have been happy with his plans. But something earthshaking had happened to her.

Never being with Stavros again was anathema to her.

If only Sakis hadn't asked him to come to his office—if only her boss hadn't called her in at the same time—then Andrea wouldn't have wound up at Stavros's villa. But she *had* come. There was only one explanation. She'd fallen madly in love with him. It was as simple and painful as that.

She knew Stavros was attracted to her, but she had no idea how deep his feelings ran. He'd just come out of another relationship. Had his mother sent Tina to Stavros's villa because she believed Tina and was upset he hadn't answered Tina's calls or texts?

Had his mother suspected Andrea would be here? Did she hope Andrea would stay away from Stavros when she heard the news about the pregnancy? Would a mother do that? Andrea didn't know, but she didn't want to believe his mother would be that calculating.

As for Tina, Andrea had seen for herself that the Grecian beauty would do anything for Stavros's affection. Was she so in love with him, she'd come to the villa on her own because she couldn't help herself? Had this kind of thing happened to Stavros in the past with other women?

If so, it could explain why he was still a bachelor. Maybe her father's bad experience in Venezuela was the reason he hadn't remarried. When there was no truth in it, how could any man ever trust in love, let alone marriage, after an exhibition like Ms. Nasso had put on tonight?

But what if Stavros was lying? She'd told him she'd withhold judgment, but that took a lot of faith.

Confused, bewildered, she got back in bed with an aching heart and pulled the covers over her shoulders, not knowing what to think. Ten more days would fly by, then no more Stavros. Maybe it was just as well. Just leave Greece before she got in too far over her head. But that was a joke.

She turned on her stomach and buried her wet face in the pillow.

The next thing she knew, it was morning. Crying herself to sleep had been one way of bringing on oblivion. But she'd awakened with the same pain, knowing her time with Stavros was growing shorter by the minute. She checked her watch. It was ten after nine.

One look in the bathroom mirror and she did what she could to repair the damage before getting dressed. After brushing her hair, she slipped into white denims and a short-sleeved powder blue T-shirt. She'd just finished tying her white sneakers when Stavros rapped on her bedroom door.

"Andrea? Are you up?"

Ridiculous how the sound of his voice thrilled her. She reached for her purse and opened the door to the exciting man dressed in a black polo and jeans. Anything she might have said got blocked in her throat because of the way he was looking at her.

"You look beautiful."

Heart attack. He was the one who was beautiful in that male way. "I don't think you're awake yet, but thank you."

His eyes narrowed on her mouth. "I've been wide awake for quite a while waiting for you. If you think I'm paying lip service, then take another look in the mirror. The color of your top has enhanced the blue of your eyes."

She got this suffocating feeling in her chest. "I can smell coffee."

"I'm good at coffee and toast. It's waiting for us out on the patio."

"Admit you're afraid I'm going to have another hunger attack. I've had several embarrassing moments in my life because of my stomach."

A chuckle followed her through the hallway and alcove to the patio, where they were treated to another glorious day of sunshine. He'd prepared eggs and fruit too. A feast. When they sat down to eat, she decided there wasn't anything he couldn't do.

Andrea ate a second helping of eggs. "You're such a great cook, I'd hire you to be mine if I could afford you."

"Let's talk about that after we go for a Jeep ride. I want to show you something."

She'd only been teasing, but his unexpected remark sounded serious and sent a curious shiver down her spine. "I'm ready to leave whenever you are." But first she got up and took their dishes to the kitchen.

"Leave them. I spoke to Raisa. She'll be in later."

"It will only take a minute."

"But *I* can't wait that long."

She flicked him a glance, thinking he was being playful, but the hard set of his jaw wiped away that notion. Without saying anything to him, she went back to the patio for her purse, then followed him out the rear entrance of the house to his Jeep.

He'd left the bedroll and blankets in the backseat. The sight of them brought back haunting memories of that first night with him. With that inscrutable expression on his face, Andrea couldn't tell if he was remembering or not. Aware of her accelerated pulse, she climbed in the front seat and attached the lap belt.

Stavros's near sleepless night had put him in a dark place. The idea that Andrea would be leaving Greece in two months had changed the timing on the playing field. He drove them out to the main road, heading in the opposite direction from the quarry.

"Where are we going?"

The breeze teased her hair. Each golden strand caught the light. "To the other side of my property."

"You mean we're still on it?"

"The villa and the swath of woods on your right are mine. Beyond them lies my future."

She shifted in her seat toward him. "That sounded cryptic."

He studied her profile. "Do you remember us talking about our dreams?"

"How could I forget?"

"I'm going to show you another one of mine, although it's in its embryo stage. Every bit of money I earned growing up, I invested so that one day I could be independent. You'd have to belong to a family like mine to understand where I'm coming from."

"It doesn't take a lot of imagination to realize you want to be your own man."

He breathed in deeply. "As you heard from my mother, last week I claimed my independence when I resigned at the board meeting. The Konstantinos family doesn't own me anymore. Best of all, I don't owe them."

He felt her speculative gaze on him while he made a turn to the right and followed the mountain road to an area of cleared land. It housed a cluster of new buildings, flatbed trucks and other machinery.

Stavros brought the Jeep to a halt at the front entrance of the office building. "Welcome to Mount Ypsarion Enterprises."

She looked all around. "This isn't a quarry."

"No. That's my family's business."

Her eyes flew to his. "What's *your* business?"

"That six-thousand-square-meter plant you see is putting out forty-five tons per hour of a new product I call Marma-Kon. It's made from those mounds of marble waste dumps behind the buildings."

"Waste?"

"Refuse from the cutting of the marble blocks. The

idea came to me years ago when I visited the different quarries and saw the wasted marble. I began talking to a group of independent chemical engineers like myself from Kavala."

"I didn't know you were an engineer like my dad."

Everything got down to her dad. Her hero worship of him meant they had a very strong bond. Ferrante had wanted her enough that he was willing to give up his own career to be with Andrea and her father. Had Andrea pressured him? Or had Ferrante loved her beyond reason and known it was the only way he could have a life with her?

"It was necessary if I hoped to build a business. Together, my engineering friends and I brainstormed about what could be done with the residue because no one was interested in the waste. In time, we came up with various products used to make dry mortars, glues and tile adhesives that are superior to those on the market because of their marble base. They're ideal for every application.

"After successfully testing the products with building contractors and architects, we saw the great potential and formed Mount Ypsarion Enterprises. From that moment on, I began negotiating with quarries all over northern Greece to buy their waste for a nominal fee and bring it here by the truckload to be processed. We house the finished products in bags and place them in those warehouses, ready for delivery by truck, train or ship."

She shook her head. "That's incredible, Stavros. Utterly incredible and it's all brand-new. Can I see inside your office first?"

"You want to?"

"Of course."

They both got out of the Jeep. Using the remote, Stavros let them inside the one-story office building. He walked her past the front desk of the main foyer to his own suite. "This is my secretary's office. Further down the hall my colleagues, Theo and Zander, have their suites with their own secretaries. If my projections are correct, this will be the first of other plants we plan to build in Penteli, near Athens, and in the Cyclades."

She swung around and smiled at him. "You planned all this."

"Along with my partners."

"But you thought of it first. You're brilliant."

He was touched by her earnestness, but he flashed her a dry smile. "A brilliant financial disaster, you mean, if my marketing projections for thirty thousand tons a year of product aren't met. Only time will tell. I and the two-hundred-plus workers we've hired could lose everything. I won't have anyone to blame but myself."

"You won't fail. You *couldn't*."

He'd needed Andrea in his life for a long time. Years, in fact…

"Such faith deserves a reward. I asked Raisa to have the hamper packed by the time we return. We'll go back to the house for it and our bathing suits. Then we'll drive to Thassos and take my speedboat. There's a secluded beach close by I know you'll love."

"I can't wait, but could I see inside the plant first? My dad was pleased when I told him your company had given permission for the tours to visit your quarry. But he'll be more than impressed when I tell him about your brainchild. It's hard to impress him."

With a work ethic like her father's, Stavros could believe it. But he was troubled by their conversation because her dad figured in it more and more. Stavros led her back outside and used the remote to activate the electronic lock. They walked to the plant in the distance and he let her inside.

One would have thought Andrea was a child on Christmas morning. But instead of exclaiming about the presents, she marveled over the up-to-date technology installed. "Would you mind if I took a few pictures with my phone to send to my father? Or would you think I'm an industrial spy?"

"I'll give you the benefit of the doubt like you gave me last night."

He noticed she let that remark go. "Dad would enjoy seeing them."

"You think?"

"I promise. He's taken me to gold mining refineries all over the world, many of them old and needing a lot of work. Trust me. This is the most elegant plant I've ever seen in my life." She lifted a beaming face to him. "You must be ecstatic. I want a couple of pictures of you too. Smile."

He did her bidding, but his patience had worn thin. "I think that's enough photos for now. Put your phone away." Stavros had only one thing on his mind. Unable to resist, he cupped her flushed cheeks in his hands and kissed her warmly on that enticing mouth of hers. "Seeing this place through your eyes is my reward," he whispered, then kissed her again, deeply this time.

A tiny moan escaped her throat as he pulled her into his body. She fit in his arms so perfectly, it was as if she were made for him. One kiss grew into more until he lost count. When he finally lifted his head so she could breathe, they were swaying together. "You have no idea how much I've wanted to do this. From the first moment we met, it's all I've been able to think about."

"Don't say anything more." He saw a tortured look enter those blue eyes as she eased out of his arms. "I was afraid this would happen if I flew to Thassos with you."

"But you came with me anyway because you couldn't help yourself, so don't bother to deny it."

She averted her eyes. "I'm not. But it scares me to have feelings like this so soon after meeting you. You're the first man since Ferrante. Our relationship took time to grow. Where you're concerned, I don't know if I can trust what's happening to me. I feel out of control."

Andrea must have been reading his mind, but he could see it had cost her a lot to admit that. "I'm not going to apologize for kissing you. If you're afraid of being with me, then I'll ask my pilot to fly you back to Thessaloniki once we reach the house. I can't blame you after what happened last night with Tina. Are you ready to go?"

Without looking at him, she nodded and started for the entrance. He let them out, then set the lock and they walked back to the Jeep. A few minutes ago he'd had a little taste of heaven, but only a taste before everything had changed. Stavros couldn't put time back to the way it was before he'd given in to his desire and kissed her. Her passionate response had set him on fire. He was still burning. *Out of control* didn't cover it.

They rode back to the villa in silence. Before he got out of the Jeep, he reached for his cell phone. She turned toward him with an anxious expression. "Who are you calling?"

"My pilot."

"Please don't, Stavros. I'm not afraid of you. You *know* I'm not."

"Maybe you should be," he bit out. "I can't give you proof that I never made love to Tina."

"I've chosen to believe you. What I think we should do is go to the beach for a good swim. I could use the exercise."

Relief swept through him that she didn't want to run away yet. "Then let's hurry. Last one to make it back to the Jeep has to pay a penalty."

"It won't be me!" Stavros could almost hear a giggle as she darted toward the house in search of her swimsuit. He used his remote to unlock the door for her, then called out, "Want to make a bet?"

He'd come prepared and was already wearing his suit under his jeans. After bounding up the steps, he hurried into the kitchen and carried the hamper down to the Jeep. To his surprise, she wasn't far behind.

After he put the hamper in the backseat, he caught her in his arms so she couldn't climb in front. "I'm afraid you'll have to pay me now."

He could feel her trembling. "You don't play fair."

"I know," he whispered. "Give me your mouth, Andrea. I'm aching for you."

"Stavros—"

Her lips slowly opened to the pressure of his. In the next breath he was lost in sensation after sensation as she gave herself up to him. Never had he known hunger like this. She couldn't seem to get enough either.

He braced his back against the door and lifted her closer so there was no air separating them. In another minute, he was going to carry her into the house and not come out again. But he had to slow down or he really would scare her away.

Forcing himself to come to his senses, he broke off kissing her and removed his hands from her arms. Like him, she fought for breath and backed away. He turned to open the front passenger door for her. "It's a good thing one of us has to drive." His voice sounded thick, even to him.

Andrea moved past him and climbed inside without saying anything. She didn't have to. Her eyes had glazed over and he could see the pulse throbbing at the base of her throat. If he put his lips to it, he wouldn't be able to stop. Summoning his willpower, he closed the door and walked around to his side of the Jeep.

"I'm glad it's you at the wheel, Stavros." Her tremulous voice gave her away even more. "I couldn't possibly function the way I'm feeling."

"I'm not sure *I* can." He locked the house with his remote, then turned on the ignition and they were off. "You realize we have Darren Lewis to thank for our condition."

"I was thinking the very same thing while we were inside your plant."

He inhaled sharply. "When I got the call from Gus, I'd just come from the board meeting. His news was the last thing I needed to hear. If you want to know the truth, before I knew your identity, I was jealous of Georgios, who'd been traveling around on the tour bus with the gorgeous American schoolteacher."

She stirred restlessly in the seat. "Georgios is happily married with a grown family."

"When you introduced yourself, I was thankful that I was happily *unmarried* and could pursue you. After you asked to come with me, I took advantage of your gift. Otherwise I would have shown up at your tour company with an excuse that I needed to talk to you."

She flicked him a glance. "It shocked me when I saw you in Sakis's office yesterday."

"After what we shared, did you really think I would let you get away from me?"

Andrea lowered her head. "I didn't know."

"Something extraordinary is happening to us. I know you feel it."

"That's the problem. In ten days I'll be leaving for Brazil with Dad."

Brazil? He almost went off the road. "What do you mean? You said you were leaving for Indonesia in two months!"

"Dad's plans were changed. You were right about the unrest there. After this weekend, I don't plan to spend any more time with you. So if you'd rather I went back to Thessaloniki tonight, I would understand."

He'd been ready for that. "I have a much better idea. Why don't we enjoy the rest of this day and forget everything else, including deadlines. I haven't had a true vacation in ages and would like to celebrate the end of my career at the Konstantinos Corporation with you. Is that too much to ask?"

His question was met with silence.

He realized she was trying to stop things before they went any further, but it was too late. It had been too late from the moment they'd met. The thought of her leaving Greece, leaving him, was too horrendous to imagine.

CHAPTER FIVE

"WE'RE IN LUCK, ANDREA. The tourists haven't come to this secluded stretch of beach yet. Those with boats will arrive later in the day in droves, but for now they prefer umbrellas and drinks available on the other side of that headland."

Andrea was delighted. A quick five-minute ride from the marina in Thassos and they had this island paradise to themselves with its backdrop of lush vegetation. Once he cut the engine, the blue-and-white boat drifted onto fine white sand.

After peeling off her clothes to reveal a two-piece white bathing suit, she jumped off the rear of the boat into aqua-blue water. Eighty-degree weather had warmed it close to bathtub temperature.

"This is heavenly, Stavros!"

While treading water, she tried not to be obvious as she watched him strip down to his black suit. It rode low on his hips. Without clothes, he could be Adonis come to life, perfect in coloring and form.

Like lightning he entered the water and reached her in seconds. A brilliant white smile was the first thing she noticed when he lifted his head close to her.

With his black hair slicked back, he was so dangerously appealing, her breath caught.

Beguiled by the sight of him, she ducked beneath the water and started swimming away from him. But when she came up for air, he was right there in front of her. From then on began an hour game of hide-and-seek with him the hunter and her the prey.

"Stop!" she begged, laughing, every time she surfaced to find him blocking her way. "It's my turn to chase you."

"Come right ahead," he challenged, but stayed where he was.

"You have to try to get away."

"What if I don't want to?" He was waiting for her to swim right into him.

"You're impossible." Exhausted by so much exertion, she did an about-face and started to head for shore when she saw a roundish shape moving beneath the water. "Stavros!" she cried. "I think a stingray is out here!"

Somehow, she didn't know how, he was right there beside her, putting himself between her and the menace. "Keep swimming like hell for the beach and shuffle your legs hard." *His* legs moved like pistons, churning the water.

They hadn't been swimming that far out. But it felt like an eternity before her feet touched sand and she collapsed on the beach out of breath. Stavros knelt down next to her and turned her over. "Are you all right?" His voice sounded unsteady.

Andrea would never forget the anxiety in his eyes. "I'm fine. What about you?"

"We got out of the way in time. Thank God you

spotted it and are an excellent swimmer, or you'd be on your way to the hospital. I haven't seen a stingray in these parts for at least four years. Their sting isn't fatal, but it can make you sick."

"I know. My dad got stung in the foot by one—years ago at Kourou beach in French Guiana. He was in bed for several days. I was so worried about him, I stayed home from school so I could take care of him."

He traced the shape of her mouth with his finger. "I'm sure that helped him get well in a hurry. Now that you've brought his name up, I'm curious to know something. Why did you and Ferrante plan to live with your father once you were married?"

"Because he's alone and doesn't have anyone else. Ferrante came from a big family and understood why I felt the way I did. Dad and I had never been separated. Stavros, I'll never be able to repay him for everything he's done for me throughout my entire life. But let's not talk about me.

"You put yourself in danger by shielding me just now." Her heart was in her throat. "How am I ever going to thank you?" She sat up and kissed his strong jaw. But what started out to be an outpouring of her gratitude turned into something else as he lowered her to the sand. Once he'd found her mouth, he began kissing her in earnest.

Those powerful legs of his entwined with hers. She clung to his hard, muscled body, craving the contact of skin against skin. One long kiss grew into another. His lips roved over her face and throat, filling her with rapture she'd never known before.

"Do you have any idea how much I want you?" He kissed her again with almost primitive force. It unleashed passion in her she didn't know herself capable of. Andrea felt on fire and kissed him back just as hungrily. He was fast becoming her addiction.

Before she lost complete control, she buried her face in his neck. "We need to slow down, Stavros. It frightens me because I've never felt this way before, not even with Ferrante."

He was a beautiful specimen of manhood, but there was so much more to him than the physical. For Stavros to find her attractive enough to want a relationship with her constituted something of a miracle. She was no femme fatale, yet he'd kissed her as if she was the most important thing in his life.

But the truth had to be faced. There was no good time for them. He'd launched a new multimillion-dollar business here on the island. She'd be leaving Greece shortly. The situation with Tina wasn't going to go away. Besides a ton of work at the office in Thessaloniki, she had packing to do and still needed to talk to her landlord and Sakis.

To go on trying to work things out with Stavros when they could find the time to fit it in made absolutely no sense. All it would do was prolong the agony. After losing Ferrante, she couldn't go through that kind of pain again. Better to cut things off now before they became any more involved. Soon they'd be on opposite sides of the world.

It was a long time before Stavros spoke. "Fear is the last emotion I want you to feel." She felt energy shoot through him before he rolled away from her and got to his feet. "What we need is to enjoy the lunch Raisa packed for us."

The moment was bittersweet because she didn't

want him to stop kissing her. At the same time, she marveled over his self-control because she didn't have any. Slowly, she sat up, but it was difficult because the desire she felt for him had dazed her. "We look like we've been bathing in sand."

"We'll wash off next to the boat. Come on." He reached for her hand and helped her all the way up. Together, they walked across the sand into the shallows. The next thing she knew, he'd swung her up in his arms as if she were a bride.

"No—Stavros!" Her protest came out on a nervous laugh as he waded deeper. "What are you going to do?"

"Give us a proper bath."

"No—" she squealed again, but by then they were both immersed.

"There." He smiled broadly after bringing them back up. "That wasn't so bad. Now our sandwiches won't taste of grit. Let's see if we've gotten all of it off your lips." Once again, Stavros started kissing her as if his life depended on it and carried her to the boat. She moaned when he finally relinquished her mouth and lowered her onto a banquette.

"I don't know about you, but that swim for our lives gave me an appetite. Kissing you has made me even more ravenous." In one deft masculine move, he levered himself inside the boat. "We're safe here, Andrea. The only thing that's going to take a bite out of you now is me."

After kissing her thoroughly once more, she felt exposed with his all-seeing eyes roving over her figure. Better put on her T-shirt. It wouldn't hurt to fix her hair either. She reached in her purse for a comb while he opened the hamper. Soon, they dug in to tasty finger food and fruit.

When Andrea had eaten all she could, she sat back and lifted her face to the sun. "This is one of those moments I'll treasure forever. Out of all the islands I've visited in the Aegean, Thassos is my favorite. Think of all the conquerors and invaders who have left their mark here. I can see why you wanted to make your home here. You have it all. Mountains, beaches, the sun, the perfect climate. It's like your own fairyland nestled in the greenery." After a pause, she said, "I have a confession to make."

He darted her a curious glance. "What's that?"

"One of the commandments says, 'Thou shalt not covet.' As I was standing on your patio, looking out over this glorious spot of earth, I understood its meaning for the first time. When you climbed the mountain, no wonder you claimed this place for your own. To live where you live really is paradise on earth. Your mythical Greek gods must be jealous of you."

Stavros stared out at the water. "I haven't needed the gods to cause me trouble. The family I was born into has made enough mischief."

"At one time or other I think most people have said that about their families."

"But there are degrees of mischief."

"Stavros? Was it always hard for you?"

He nodded. "Pretty much from day one. I didn't want to do things the way my father did. He wanted me in private school. I wanted to go to public school. He didn't like my close friends who weren't good enough for him. He didn't like me dating a lot of girls. I went through them like water."

"Was there one you fell hard for?"

"All of them."

"Be serious."

"I am. I never went with someone I wasn't crazy about."

"For a time, you mean."

He grinned.

"How long did the attraction last?" she asked.

"Maybe two dates."

"I was the same way," Andrea confessed. "I never had myriads of boyfriends, but I liked guys a lot better than girls."

"Your only problem was that none of them measured up to your dad except Ferrante."

"It wasn't like that, Stavros. I never compared him to Dad. What I loved about Ferrante was his gentle nature, and that's one of Dad's best qualities. But in other ways they were completely different."

Stavros made an odd sound in his throat. "My father has never kept his opinions to himself. He didn't like my doing jobs for anyone but him. I was happy for any job that would help me save money and get away from him micromanaging me. He had his mind made up I would go to college in London for a business degree. I decided I wanted to be an engineer and went to MIT. He wanted me to live in Thessaloniki with the rest of the family. I wanted to live here on Thassos.

"We disagreed on every issue. He let me know when he thought it was time for me to get married. I told him I wasn't sure that day would ever come. He'd picked out Tina to be the woman I should marry. The

Nassos came from the right bloodline with all the important connections and affluence."

"Does your mother have no say in how you conduct your life?"

"She mostly goes along with my father, especially where Tina is concerned. But I think that of all my decisions, choosing to live on Thassos has caused her the most grief. Mother sees us like a clan, all closely knit. I'm afraid I'm a person who needs more breathing room."

Andrea pondered everything, almost afraid to ask her next question. "Has there ever been a time when you and your father agreed on something important?"

"Yes. He supported me when I played soccer. When the board proposed new names for vice president of the corporation, we both felt that my brother, Leon, had the stability and wisdom to be the best choice over my two cousins."

"That's it?"

"I'm sure there were a few other times, but not many. That's something you can't comprehend, can you?"

"No…but then I'm not a man."

His smile was devilish. "I'm happy to say you're the personification of femininity."

"Be serious for a minute."

"I'm trying, but it's hard when I'm looking at you."

It was hard on her when his eyes seemed to devour her. "Did your brother pick his own wife?"

"Yes, but she had the right breeding and family history to satisfy my parents. Leon gets along without making waves. He's a terrific father to their children. I manage to do things that get under my father's skin.

It's not on purpose. I love my father because he's my father. But I don't like him very much. Can you understand that?"

"I guess I can, but it makes me sad. Dad and I just click."

Stavros nodded. "Otherwise you wouldn't be leaving Greece with him."

She averted her eyes. "How does your father treat Leon's children?"

"He's still dictatorial, but a little nicer."

"Then there's hope. I've told you before that I think you'll make a wonderful father, Stavros. Maybe it'll take giving your dad some grandchildren to soften him."

In the midst of their conversation Andrea heard music. She turned her head and saw that a cabin cruiser had discovered their special spot. People were on board playing loud music, disturbing the tranquillity. In the far distance, she saw a sailboat coming closer.

She and Stavros hadn't come back to the boat any too soon. A little earlier and the sight of the two of them wrapped in each other's arms on the sand would have provided unexpected entertainment for anyone watching. Heat swept through her body as she remembered how expertly Stavros had brought her alive. Andrea still felt alive and he wasn't even touching her.

"Our paradise has been invaded," Stavros murmured. "No more isolation for us." All of a sudden, he closed the hamper and got up, unaware of her private thoughts. He stood there shirtless in the hot sun while the breeze blew his black hair away from his forehead. There couldn't be a more fabulous man alive.

"It's time to leave. Besides the overcrowding, you've gotten enough sun. Put your life jacket back on, Andrea." She'd forgotten, but he never forgot anything to make her comfortable or safe. "I'll jump out and push us off."

Something was bothering him, but she couldn't read his mind. Already she regretted he was bringing this glorious outing to a close. With what looked like effortless male agility, Stavros got out to move the boat into deeper water. It took a lot of strength, though he made it look like child's play. In a minute, he came around the driver's side to climb back on.

But as he started to get in, she heard a groan. He managed to make it inside the boat, but he sank to the floor, grabbing his lower leg. His features contorted in pain.

"Turn over on your stomach, Stavros."

Groaning again, he made a great effort to do as she'd asked. Andrea hunkered down and noticed immediately the small cut just above his ankle. The bleeding was minimal. "I don't believe it. That stingray got you. This looks like the cut on Dad's foot. Don't move. I'm phoning for help."

She lunged for her purse and pulled out her cell phone to call emergency services. Stavros was already losing color.

The second the dispatcher answered, she said, "This is Despinis Linford. Send an ambulance to the private boat dock at Thassos marina ASAP. Kyrie Stavros Konstantinos has been stung by a stingray above the back of the ankle. He'll be in a blue-and-white speedboat. I'll blast the horn to help you spot him. Hurry!"

"Andrea," he muttered when she clicked off. "You shouldn't have told them my name." She could tell he was barely holding on because of the pain.

She got behind the wheel of the boat and turned on the engine. "Everyone knows who you are. I did it to get you the best care immediately." She backed the boat around, then put the gear in forward and they shot away from the beach. The marina was just around the headland.

"Hang on, Stavros. You'll be out of your pain soon." Andrea thanked providence that they hadn't gone to some beach farther away where help wouldn't be available as fast.

Once she'd rounded the point, she headed straight for the boat dock. To her joy, she saw an ambulance drawing near. She pressed on the horn and kept pressing. After lowering her speed, she cut the engine and allowed the boat to slide into its private berth. The ambulance attendants came running with a gurney. A crowd of people had assembled, wanting to know what was going on.

"Take good care of him," she begged as they lifted him out of the boat.

"I'll be fine, Andrea." His voice sounded weak.

"I know you will. I'll come to the medical center in a few minutes."

She watched him being put in the ambulance. After it drove off, she slipped on her denims. Then she gathered up his clothes. The keys to the house and Jeep were in his pocket. She pulled them out and put them in her purse along with the boat key. Andrea would have to leave the hamper for now.

One of the bystanders tied up the boat for her. She thanked him before heading for the Jeep in the parking area.

There were signs leading to the medical center, but she knew where it was because she'd checked it out as part of her job, in case of emergencies on the tour here. She found a parking space near the ER entrance and rushed inside. The staff person in triage needed information. Andrea told her what she could.

"Are you a relative?"

"No. A friend. How soon can I go in to see him?"

"Let me call the desk."

Andrea waited ten minutes in agony before she was allowed through the doors to his curtained cubicle. Stavros, dressed in a hospital gown, lay there with his eyes closed. The middle-aged ER doctor smiled at her. "Despinis Linford?" She nodded. "I'm Dr. Goulas. Come in. I understand you're the heroine who got our island's most famous resident here in record time."

Andrea knew Stavros was revered. "I tried. How is he?"

"We're already giving him pain medication through the drip. He's drifting in and out of sleep. The pain from that sting has traveled up his limb and could last forty-eight hours. I've checked his vital signs. Kyrie Konstantinos is doing well. I've given him a tetanus shot to be on the safe side.

"What we're going to do now is soak his lower leg in hot water for about an hour. That reduces a lot of the pain. Then I'll inject more painkiller around the cut and take a look to see if there's any foreign matter before I sew it up."

She took a shaky breath. "Can I stay in here with him?"

"I'd like you to. When he was brought in, his greatest concern was you. It will ease his mind to know he can see and talk to you. Why don't you sit down? This has been an ordeal for you too."

Andrea nodded and took a seat in one of the chairs. "We'd seen the stingray earlier, but it was out in deeper water. I couldn't believe it had come in right by his boat."

"They hide in the shallows under the sand."

"Stavros must have stepped on it while he was pushing the boat off the sand. I heard him groan and then he paled so fast."

"It's the shock. But the cut doesn't appear to be deep and I doubt it will become infected."

"Can I take him home tonight?"

"If his blood pressure is good and he doesn't have any trouble breathing, then I would say that's a real possibility. He'll have to stay on oral antibiotics for a while." Her father had been given antibiotics too.

While she sat there waiting for Stavros to wake up, she could tell he was getting his color back, thank heaven. In a minute, a technician wheeled in a cart holding a rectangular basin of hot water. The doctor lifted Stavros's left leg. Once the basin was in place, he lowered the bottom half and foot into the water.

Stavros was such a striking man. To see him incapacitated…to see one of those long, strong legs injured…it just killed her.

"There's a lounge on the other side of the clinic with food and drinks."

"Thank you, but I'm not hungry. We'd just eaten a big meal before this happened."

"Very good. I'll be back."

"Thank you for everything, Doctor."

"It's a privilege."

That was the sentiment Andrea saw in the people who interacted with Stavros. She loved him so much and pulled the chair closer to his side where she wouldn't disturb the drip in his hand. Her mind played over the events of the past ten days. It was pure chance that they'd met at all.

If Sakis hadn't sent her to investigate Darren's disappearance—if the teen had decided to run away at another stop on the tour—if Stavros hadn't been available. So many ifs that had to occur with split-second timing for them to have been brought together in the cosmos.

And now this injury.

It could have been fatal if he'd been stung in the heart or abdomen. A shudder ran through her body. While she sat there trying not to think about his close call, the doctor came in again, followed by the technician, who wheeled in another basin of hot water. They repeated the process.

"His vital signs are holding," the doctor informed her. "This sleep is doing him good. I'll give this another twenty minutes, then take a look at the cut."

Ten more minutes and she heard him say her name. "I'm here, Stavros."

"I need to feel you." He moved his hand toward

her. When she grasped it, his heavily lashed eyelids opened.

Andrea leaned closer. "How's the pain now?"

"What pain?"

She squeezed his hand. "You don't have to act brave around me."

"Whatever they gave me knocked me out. I don't feel a thing."

"That's good."

"Have I told you you're the most amazing woman I've ever known?"

"It takes an amazing man to recognize one."

"I'm serious."

"So am I." She smiled. "Your doctor says it's an honor to be taking care of you. I agree. Is there anyone who ought to know what's happened to you?"

"The only person of importance is you. With you watching over me, I don't want anyone else."

"That's the painkiller talking."

"Andrea—" He tugged on her hand. "You're not really going to Brazil with your father, are you?"

Her breath caught. "Let's not talk about that right now. You need to rest and let the medication work."

"You can't go. We've only started getting to know each other."

If only he knew the pain she was in just thinking about it. "Right now, you need to concentrate on getting better."

"Don't change the subject." His grip on her hand was surprisingly strong. He would have said more, but the doctor and the technician walked in, interrupting him.

"Let's take a look at the cut." He eyed Andrea.

"We have to turn him over. If you'll step out, this won't take long."

"I want her to come right back," Stavros stated in what she considered had to be his boardroom voice.

Dr. Goulas smiled at her. "Is that your wish too?"

"Yes. Please."

"Then stay outside the curtain. I'll tell you when you can come in again."

Stavros's grip on her hand tightened before he released her. She welcomed the pressure. They had a connection that was growing stronger every minute.

When she'd asked him if she could call someone in his family to let them know he was in the clinic, he'd said no. His history with his father haunted her. When she thought of her own relationship with her dad, her heart bled for Stavros because he hadn't had a loving experience.

Ten minutes passed before she was called back in.

"Come over here, Andrea." Stavros reached for her hand.

"Good news," the doctor said. "I've cleaned the wound and put in some stitches. This should heal nicely."

"How soon can I be released?" Stavros wanted to know.

"Let's finish out the drip. Then I'll want to check your blood pressure. If you remain stabilized, you'll be able to go home this evening, but it will be bed rest until Monday. I'll send an antibiotic with you, and I'll want to see you again on Friday to check the wound."

Andrea sensed the doctor was about to leave and eased her hand from Stavros's grip.

"Where do you think you're going?" he demanded.

How she loved him! "I'll be right back." She hurried to catch up with the doctor outside the curtain. "Dr. Goulas? Thank you more than I can say."

He nodded. "Kyrie Konstantinos is a very important man, but his type makes the worst kind of patient. See that he stays down and follows directions. If you can stop him from going to work on Monday, that would be best. Between you and me, he's not out of the woods yet. Follow-up care with this kind of wound is critical to make certain there's no recurring infection."

"I know. My father received a similar sting on his foot years ago and was absolutely impossible."

"I take it he's an important man too."

"Very, especially to me."

He patted her arm. "The more sleep our patient gets right now, the better. I'll be around again later."

When Andrea peeked inside the curtain, Stavros's eyes were closed. Taking the doctor's advice to heart, she walked through to the other side of the clinic for some coffee. Today's experience had taken a toll. Some caffeine would give her energy for what lay ahead.

Taking advantage of the time, she phoned her boss. It went through to his voice mail. Andrea left the message about Stavros's ordeal and explained she needed to nurse him for a little while. Would it be all right if she didn't come in to work until Tuesday? If the answer was yes, then Sakis didn't need to call her back.

Next, she phoned her landlord and left the message that she'd be vacating the apartment within ten days to travel with her father to Brazil. But she would pay the money still owed to honor the lease.

Thinking of her father, she sent him the photos she'd taken of Stavros's new plant. She texted an explanation so he'd understand what he was looking at, but she stopped short of sending him pictures of Stavros. She explained about the missing teen and the opportunity to see the plant before she returned to Thessaloniki.

On her way back to the ER, she went to the restroom and was horrified to see how bad she looked. She needed to shower and wash the sand out of her hair. But all that would have to come later after she'd driven him home.

She freshened up the best she could and went back to look in on Stavros, pleased to see he was no longer hooked up to the drip. To her surprise, he was awake. One of the staff must have helped him to dress in his jeans and polo shirt. His penetrating gray eyes centered on her.

"I wondered when you were going to come back. I'm good to go home. They're bringing a wheelchair."

"In that case, I'll go out to the Jeep and pull it around."

"If you want to know the truth, I'm glad this happened."

Andrea sucked in her breath. "How can you say that after being in a life-and-death situation?"

"Because before I got stung, I knew you were going to ask me to send for the helicopter so you could leave for Thessaloniki tonight."

She looked away. He knew her better than she knew herself. "I'll see you out in front."

Her heart was at war between the two most wonderful men in the world. She loved both of them, but owed her dad everything. Her desire to be with Stavros for as long as he still desired her was selfish. When her dad had worked so hard for them all his life, how could she say goodbye to him and stay in Greece knowing he was facing the future alone? He had no one else.

Andrea walked out of the clinic to the Jeep, oblivious to her surroundings because a sadness had taken hold of her, one she couldn't throw off. It wasn't like the pain after Ferrante's death. That had been final. She'd finally gotten over it because she knew he'd never come back.

But Stavros was vibrantly alive despite that awful stingray's sting.

No matter how many thousands of miles separated them, she'd be tormented by the knowledge that he was here and she'd walked away from him. Not because she'd wanted to.

But because she had to.

A few minutes later she saw a male staff member wheeling him out of the ER exit in a wheelchair. After the vision she'd had of him lying in the bottom of the boat writhing in pain, to see him looking this good caused her heart to skip a beat. You'd never know his jeans covered a potentially serious wound.

After helping him climb in the Jeep, the orderly came around and handed her a plastic bag. In a whisper, he said, "He's a little dizzy." She nodded. Inside the bag was a packet of dressings and two kinds of pills. She thanked the orderly and put it on the backseat.

Turning to the man she adored, she said, "Ready to go home?"

"As long as you come with me."

Now her pulse was racing. "I won't abandon you. I promise." She pulled out of the ER driveway, onto the road, and headed for the road that would take them past Panagia to his villa.

"I'm going to hold you to that." His vaguely fierce tone sent a shiver through her.

"Try to relax against the seat and sleep until we get there."

"I've been sleeping on and off for hours. Tell me how you learned to do everything so well."

"What do you mean?"

"You drove us away from that beach without a hitch and you handle this Jeep like you've been driving one all your life."

"My father's work meant he lived in some pretty remote, out-of-the-way places. He needed a four-wheel drive to get anywhere on unpaved roads. I had to learn fast. When we took little vacations, we usually headed for water anywhere we could find it. Dad loves to fish. We rented a lot of different kinds of boats. I drove while he looked for the best spots."

His hand squeezed her shoulder. "Because of your expertise at everything, you saved me from going into irreversible shock. I don't know another woman who would have your quick thinking in a crisis and sense instinctively what to do."

"Sure you do, but you've never given them a chance. You're so self-sufficient, you're not the kind of man who gets himself into trouble he can't get out of. I just happened to be there at the exact moment you actually needed help, not that you'd ever ask for it."

"Am I that bad?" he teased.

"Worse! I guess that stingray got so mad at being foiled the first time, he came after you out of revenge."

Laughter broke from Stavros, the deep male kind that thrilled her. "How do you know it was a he?"

"I don't. It was a figure of speech, but men do love a challenge, don't they."

He laughed again. "It sounds like you've been around a lot of them."

"Living with my dad, my life's been filled with men. Mine workers, plant workers, chemists, engineers. Thousands of them," she volunteered. "Maybe even a million."

She could feel him staring at her profile. "So how on earth did you meet Ferrante?"

"My dad and I took a ski holiday in Cortina. Ferrante and I shared a chair lift. He was on vacation too. We got talking, and then he followed me down the mountain, and then followed me to the hotel where he met Dad. Before lon—"

"You were in love." Stavros filled in the rest.

"Not right away. Let's just say he was a better skier than Dad. I loved it because my dad does everything well. He'd also climbed more mountains than my father, leaving Dad and me totally impressed."

"So my little jaunt up Mount Ypsarion wouldn't make a dent in your father's estimation."

"A dent is a dent." Her reply produced a smile from him. "But I sent him the photos of your plant along with an explanation. It'll blow his mind knowing you've created a product no one else has. You have genius in you, Stavros."

"That's nice to know," came the mocking comment.

"I wasn't patronizing you." She made a turn into his private road. "We're almost to the house. I can tell you're going to need another pain pill right away. I'll pull up in front where you won't have to negotiate so many steps."

Thankful they were home, she jumped out and ran around to help him. "Put your arm around my shoulders and let me take some of your weight. You need to get off your leg as soon as possible."

He not only slid his arm around her, he pulled her against him and kissed her hungrily on the mouth. "I love my life being in your hands."

His words shook her to the foundation.

"Come on, Achilles. Let's get you into bed."

He let out a bark of laughter. "I need a shower first," he said.

"Not tonight, Stavros. The doctor said you can do it in the morning."

They made it inside and down the hall to his bedroom. She hadn't been in it before and tried not to think about it as they moved inside. "What can I do to help?"

"Take me to the bathroom."

She did his bidding and waited outside until he appeared in the doorway. Once again, she lent him her strength until they reached the bed. He let go of her long enough to unfasten his jeans. "I'll need you to pull them over my leg."

Andrea knelt down.

"I can see you're blushing. Don't worry. The hospital dried my swimming trunks before I put them back on."

"I wasn't worried."

"Liar," he whispered in a silky voice.

As soon as that was accomplished, he stood up so she could draw back the covers. Without any urging, he removed his polo shirt, then lay down on his side. She helped ease his bad leg onto the mattress. The other followed. Earlier in the day she'd been caught by those legs, loving every second of her entrapment.

By the sound of his sigh, she knew bed felt heavenly to him. "I'm going out to the Jeep to bring in the rest of our things. Be right back."

In another five minutes she'd given him two pills and tucked him in. "Here's your phone, wallet and keys. I'll put them on this side table with your water. If you need me in the night, phone me."

"It's only eight thirty. I'm not ready to go to sleep yet."

"You will be once those pills take effect. Good night."

He called to her, but she ignored him and headed for the guest bedroom. She needed a shower in the worst way. After working up a lather of shampoo, she rinsed off and emerged feeling sparkling clean.

With a towel wrapped around her hair, she went back in the bedroom and pulled a nightgown and robe from her duffel bag. It was nice feeling normal again. She padded through the house to the kitchen to get a bottle of water. As she took it out of the fridge, she heard a loud couple of knocks. The sound was coming from the back door.

Had Stavros's mother or ex-girlfriend heard about his injury? Or maybe it was Raisa.

She cinched the belt tighter on her pink-striped robe and hurried through the rear hallway to the door.

She jumped when she saw a man on the other side. He bore a superficial resemblance to Stavros. This had to be his brother. Maybe someone at the hospital had called him. She hadn't heard the helicopter because she'd been in the shower.

Andrea undid the lock. He came inside and shut the door. The way he looked at her, it was apparent he was equally shocked to see a strange woman answering the door.

"I'm Leon, Stavros's brother. And you are...?"

"No one important. It's nice to meet you."

"Likewise," he murmured. "Where's Stavros? He hasn't answered his phone all day."

"You'll find him in the bedroom, where all will be explained. If you'll excuse me, I'm going to bed myself. Be sure to lock up when you let yourself out again. He's in no condition to do it."

CHAPTER SIX

"WHAT THE HELL is going on?"

At the sound of his brother's voice, Stavros lifted his head off the pillow. Something had to be wrong for his forty-year-old brother to fly all the way from Thessaloniki at this hour.

"Leon? What are you doing here?"

"You haven't answered my phone calls all day," he accused without preamble. "I got worried and flew here because it isn't like you not to respond."

"Take a breath and I'll explain. Sit down, bro. How's your family?"

"They're fine." Leon picked up the chair and put it at the side of the bed. They were alike in coloring, but his married brother was an inch taller and carried about thirty more pounds. He grinned. "Who's the beautiful blue-eyed woman who opened the door wearing a pink-and-white-striped robe and a towel covering her hair?"

Well, well. That was a sight Stavros had yet to behold. "You mean she didn't tell you?"

"No. She said she wasn't anyone important and told me she was going to bed, would I lock up on my way out."

Stavros let go with another burst of laughter.

"What's so funny? Why *are* you in bed?"

He was glad Leon had come. The medicine had knocked him out earlier. Now he was awake and going crazy without Andrea's company. "Why don't you grab a beer from the fridge and then we'll talk."

"You don't want one?"

"I can't."

"You're not making sense."

"The doctor told me no alcohol for a while."

Leon's brows met in a frown. He leaned closer to him. "I knew something had happened to you."

"Would you believe I got stung by a stingray today? The pain was unreal. That unimportant person who answered the door saved my life."

"Is she a nurse from the clinic? Is that why she's here?"

"It's a long story."

"I've got the time."

For the next little while, Stavros explained everything. But at the mention of PanHellenic Tours, Leon made a strange sound in his throat. "Wait just a minute. This Andrea is the blonde American woman who has Mother and Tina Lasso in fits? She speaks Greek like a native. I would never have guessed."

"Try a dozen languages she's mastered. Brains and beauty."

"Despinis Linford is a knockout, all right. But she's also one of the reasons I flew here to see you tonight."

"I figured you had some bad news for me or you wouldn't have come."

"It's serious, I'm afraid. Dad's in a rage."

"That's old news. He knew I was forming my own

company. My resignation was inevitable. My company is already a week into production."

"I know, but it's not just that, Stav. He expects you to do the right thing for Tina now that she's pregnant."

"If I'd ever loved Tina, I would have married her long ago. She's bluffing, Leon. But in any case, I never slept with her, so it couldn't be mine."

"You and I both know that, but our father is beyond listening to reason. I came here to warn you. I overheard him tell Mother that if you don't marry Tina, he's going to prevent any more sales of the marble waste from our quarries to be sold to you."

"He *what*?" A pain stabbed him to the depths. His own father would really do that?

"Are you serious?"

"I'm afraid so. He'll try to shut you down in order to get his own way."

"Leon—what kind of man does such a thing to his son?"

"I'm sorry, Stav."

Tears filled Stavros's eyes, unbidden. "Father really hates me to consider betraying me like this. It's one blow I could never have anticipated." He thought back to his earlier conversation with Andrea about his father. If his father was willing to go that far, it could impact Stavros's relationship with her. Stavros didn't want this touching Andrea and would go to any lengths to keep her in his life.

Leon put a hand on his shoulder. "He doesn't hate you, Stav. If you want to know my opinion, Tina's father has put the squeeze on our father. He may even have threatened to take away the shipping services he has provided all these years."

"So I'm supposed to do the right thing by Tina?"

"It's the only way to solve the problem."

He looked in Leon's eyes. "Are *you* asking me to do it?"

"Hell, no. I couldn't marry a woman I didn't love. I wouldn't! To my way of thinking, this is pure sabotage on Nasso's part and he's railroading our father. You need to confirm the facts of Tina's so-called pregnancy first."

"She might be pregnant, Leon, but doing a DNA before the baby is born could prove dangerous to the fetus. I'd have to wait until after it's delivered before the test could be done to prove it's not mine."

His brother frowned. "That could mean six months or longer. Can you keep your new business afloat that long without suffering?"

Stavros nodded. "There are other quarries, but I'll be forced to do some fast negotiating to provide backup when the need comes. Orders are pouring in."

"Then get better and do it! I'd help you if I could."

"You already have by giving me a heads-up. I owe you. Anyway, I know your hands are tied. Tell you what, Leon. Tina's father can plot till doomsday, but he and Father aren't going to put me out of business," Stavros said icily.

"There's more."

He stared at his brother. "How could there be more?"

"Mother believes you're involved with—"

"Andrea?" Stavros supplied the name. "She'd be dead-on right."

Leon blinked. "You mean…?"

"Yes."

"But—"

"There's no but. Only *if.*"

"What are you saying?"

"If Andrea doesn't love me enough, then my life will have to go on without her. But for the life of me, I can't figure out how I'll be able to live without her."

Leon looked shocked. "I thought she saved your life."

"She did. However, there's someone else more important to her."

"More important than you?"

Stavros loved his brother for being there for him. "You have no idea."

"Who is it?"

"Picture a single father who's been all things to his motherless daughter from the day she was born. They've traveled the world and have been inseparable. At the end of this month, he's leaving for Brazil and she'll be going with him. He's got an unbreakable hold on her. It's called love."

"Then you'll just have to find a way to make her love you more. You have the power."

"Not if she fears Tina really is pregnant with my child."

"I think if she thought that, she wouldn't be here waiting on you hand and foot." He got to his feet. Stavros prayed his brother was right. "Your eyelids are drooping. I'm going to leave. The pilot's waiting for me. Take care of that wound. Don't be surprised if Tina's father has more surprises in store to hurt you."

"I'll consider myself warned."

Leon leaned down and they hugged. "Do me a

favor. Answer my phone calls from now on and keep me up to date. I'll help any way I can."

"Will do. Thanks for coming. I owe you, bro."

Stavros listened until he heard the helicopter lift off. His brother had left him with one salient thought. *You have the power.* Without hesitation, he phoned Andrea. He wasn't going to let his father drive her away. She answered on the second ring.

"I just heard your brother leave. Are you all right?"

"No. Would you mind coming to my room?"

"I'll be right there."

To his delight, she appeared in the pink-and-white-striped robe, but was minus the towel. While his brother had been here, she'd blow-dried her hair. The silky texture had natural curl and waved around her neck. She was like a delicious confection.

"Can I get you something?"

"I don't need anything, but I'd like to ask a favor of you if you're willing, and provided you can even do it. This can't wait."

"Hmm…you've got me curious." She walked over to the bed and sat on the chair Leon had placed there.

"My brother brought me unsettling news." After he'd finished telling her about his father's plan to sabotage his business, and what part Tina's father played in the whole scenario, her eyes filled with tears.

"Your own father would do that so you'll marry Tina Nasso?" Her voice shook.

"He's afraid of the consequences if I don't. He and her father have business connections in common, so he's hoping I'll cave before he has to carry out that threat. Leon came to warn me."

She shook her head. "But you're his flesh and blood."

"With a father like yours, I realize you can't comprehend it. Unfortunately, the time has come where I have to be a step ahead of mine because I've worked years to see the fruition of my business plans, As I told you earlier, if I fail, it'll be letting down my colleagues, not to mention hundreds of employees with families. I can't risk that." *Or you...*

She drew in a deep breath. "What favor do you want from me?"

"In the next few days I have to visit some quarries in Thassos not owned by my family in order to negotiate contracts for their marble refuse."

"But you're supposed to be resting your leg or it might not heal."

"That's why I need someone to drive me around and be my mouthpiece. I can't expect my colleagues to do this. I've let them know I'm laid up for a few days. In that amount of time, I can get this other work done. Is it possible your boss would give you the time off? I'll pay you for your time."

She bit her lip. "I don't want your money. You saved me from the stingray. That's payment enough. Since I'm leaving Greece so soon, I think Sakis has kind of given up on me doing much work. He would probably okay me for one more day off. I already asked him if I didn't have to come in until Tuesday."

His heart did a swift kick. "You did?"

"Yes. The doctor told me you shouldn't try to go to work before then, and he wants to see you back on Friday. But, Stavros—riding around in the Jeep would never do."

"We'll go in the Mercedes. I'll rest my leg across the backseat. By Tuesday we should have covered four or five quarries. Hopefully I'll come home with enough contracts to keep the plant running in case my father carries out his plan."

Andrea got up from the chair. "I'll phone Sakis first thing in the morning. If he's in agreement, then I'll be happy to drive you around. But tomorrow's Sunday, and you *have* to stay down."

"I'll be good."

"Ha! The doctor and I had a discussion about you."

He smiled. "What did he say?"

"It's a secret. Now, is there anything I can do for you?"

"One thing."

She shook her head. "Just not that one."

"You're still afraid of the way you feel about me." He loved it because it meant her feelings for him ran so deep.

"Good night."

When she'd gone, he turned off his lamp. At least she hadn't left him yet.

Andrea got up early and dressed in jeans and a short-sleeved, botanical-printed blouse. She hadn't heard a peep out of Stavros. After fixing him a breakfast tray, she took it through to his bedroom and discovered he wasn't in bed.

She put the tray on the dresser and waited for him to come out of the bathroom. In a few minutes, he emerged shaved and wearing a navy toweling robe. His hair was still damp from his shower. She could smell the soap.

It wasn't fair that one man should be endowed with the kind of male attributes that made a woman breathless at the very sight of him. The fact that he was limping did nothing to take away the sheer vital essence of him.

"Good morning, Stavros."

His gaze zeroed in on her. Maybe it was the color of his robe that made his gray eyes look almost black. "How long have you been waiting?"

"For just a minute. I brought breakfast for both of us. Though I'm sure that shower felt good, you need to get right back in bed. I'd like to take a look at that wound. You probably need a fresh dressing. If you'll lie facedown, this will only take a moment."

He limped to the bed and stretched out. She pulled one clean dressing from the box and leaned over to undo the old one. "There's been a little drainage, but that's to be expected. Everything looks good."

Andrea applied the new one and discarded the other one. "If you'll turn over while I wash my hands, then we'll eat." Satisfied he was able to get on his back with less difficulty than last night, she hurried into his bathroom and came right back. "If you'll make some room, I'll put the tray on the side of the bed and we'll eat."

She brought their food over. "As you see, I can make toast and coffee, just like you. I also brought you some fresh water to take your pills."

He took them first, then lay propped on his side while they ate. She'd peeled an orange and pulled the wedges apart for them. "How's the pain?"

"It's sore, but the intensity of it has gone."

"When you climbed into the boat yesterday, I could

see the pain in your face. I'm so thankful you're feeling better."

"Me too, and we both know who deserves the credit for getting me immediate help."

"Except that, in my haste, I'm afraid the hamper is still in the boat."

"No problem. I'll get it later in the week. Did you phone your boss?"

"I left him a message to call me."

"Good." When he'd finished eating, he said, "Okay. Now that we've gotten all the small talk out of the way, let's get rid of the tray."

Adrenaline filled her bloodstream. "I'll take it out. Is there anything you want me to bring you?"

"If you'd bring my laptop from the den."

"Coming right up." She hurried to the kitchen, darted to his den and returned. "Here you go." As she handed the computer to him, he pulled her down on the side of the bed where the tray had been. "Stavros—" Her heart pounded outrageously.

"What's the matter? I only want to thank you properly. Come here, Andrea."

He'd put one arm around her neck, forcing her down until their mouths fused. The unexpectedness of his action had caught her off guard. She half lay against his chest, unable to fight those seductive forces taking over her body. Her hands had a will of their own and slid into his hair. She loved its vibrancy.

"I could eat you alive," he cried softly, treating her to every kind of kiss imaginable until she was losing awareness of the surroundings. Her longing for him had reached a dangerous level of intensity. She had to fight not to go under.

"Your leg—we have to stop." She found the strength to tear her lips from his and pulled away so she could stand up. Weaving on her feet, she drank in gulps of air. "This isn't the kind of bed rest Dr. Goulas had in mind."

"Not even if it's the best medicine for me?"

She let out a laugh bordering on hysteria. "Only you would say that. You're impossible, *Kyrie* Konstantinos, so I have an idea. While you do some work, I'll drive down to the marina in the Jeep and bring the hamper back. I might as well fill the gas tank and buy a newspaper for you at the same time. You can phone if you need me. I promise to be quick."

"As long as you're going, buy me a pasteli."

"I'll get one for me too." She reached for the car keys on the nightstand. "Those sesame seed candy bars are yummy."

"So are you, Andrea. Hurry back."

Two hours later she returned, having done all her errands. She emptied the hamper, then did the few dishes and cleaned up the kitchen. With that accomplished, she hurried through the house to Stavros's bedroom with goodies. He'd propped himself on his side to work on the computer.

She put the newspaper and candy bars down next to him. His piercing gaze found hers. "You were gone so long, I was starting to worry."

Andrea laughed. "Sure you were." She sat down on the chair next to him. "What have you been working on?"

"Our trip. Did you hear from your boss yet?"

"Yes. He's rough around the edges, but has a kind heart. When he heard about your encounter with the stingray, he told me to take care of you and not worry about things at the office. Dorcas is going to fill in for me."

"I haven't heard that name before."

"She's a friend of mine who works in Accounts. Already I can tell Sakis is thinking ahead."

One side of his mouth turned up at the corner. "You have him wrapped around your little finger. Even though you haven't left him yet, inside I wager he's been mourning his loss."

She let out a sigh. "You always manage to say the right thing."

"Do I?"

"Yes. For being so nice, I've brought you another present." She pulled a packet of playing cards out of her jeans pocket. "How about a game of diloti?"

"You know how to play that?"

"Casino is the game of choice in every country where I've lived. Diloti is the Greek version of virtually the same thing. Are you up for a few rounds?"

"Watch me," he said with a satisfied gleam in his eyes.

"But we won't play for money."

"I'm way ahead of you."

Her adrenaline surged. "I bet you are, but since I intend to win, I'm not going to worry about it. We'll play until one o'clock."

"What happens then?"

"Lunch. I bought some fresh spanakopitas." She loved cheese pies more than about anything.

"I'll set my watch alarm so we have to quit at the same time."

"That's fair."

"So be it." She glimpsed fire in his eyes. "You're on!"

The race was all about winning the most points. She got lucky and made a sweep early. Then luck was on his side and he made one. As the pressure began to build, Andrea started to eat her candy. Stavros had already devoured his.

Cards had always been serious business for her. Naturally he was good. What Greek man worth his salt wasn't! So good, in fact, she feared she might lose. Andrea kept looking at her watch. Time was almost up. "I can hear your awesome brain doing calculations, Stavros. You're making me nervous."

That deep chuckle of his permeated her bones just as the alarm sounded. He checked her last play. "You can't build upon a four-join with an ace on the board and a five in your hand. I win!"

"You don't have to sound so gleeful about it." She gathered up the cards and put them back in the pack. "It's time for your pills." She handed him the water.

His smile taunted her before he swallowed his medicine. "What's the matter? You have nothing to fear from me. I'm pretty much incapacitated."

Stavros wasn't the problem. *She* was. "Come on. I'll help you to the bathroom on the condition that you behave."

A glimmer of a smile hovered on his lips. "I don't know how to do that."

Her temper flared. "Do you want help or not?"

"I do, but then I want to eat on the patio. The lounger out there is as good as this bed."

She knew he was going stir-crazy. "You're right."

Andrea offered her support and in a few minutes they reached the patio. She fixed the lounger so it lay flat. That way he could stretch out on his side. "Don't get any ideas about pulling me down with you or we'll both end up with a broken back."

His chuckle followed her as she left for the kitchen. Before long, she brought out the pies and iced tea he'd liked before. After she put his drink on the stone flooring and handed him a couple of pies, she pulled one of the chairs over and sat by him to eat.

"Uh-oh. You're facing the wrong way and can't see the coast."

"I'll be looking at it for the rest of my life, but you won't be here after a few more days, so I'd rather look at you." Stavros knew how to press on a sore wound.

"If the heat gets too much for you, tell me and I'll help you back in the house."

"Why is it you always change the subject when I mention your leaving?"

Because I'm in pain and don't want to be separated from you. "I didn't realize I did that."

He eyed her over his glass. "Where will you be living in Brazil?"

"The Serra do Ouro gold mine is near a town called Itapetim in the northeastern area. Dad says it's mostly agrarian."

"What kind of work do you think you'll do there?"

She took a long drink first. "I'll find something. We won't be there very long."

A stillness seemed to come over Stavros. "Why not?"

"Dad's tired of traveling the world. He wants to

go back to his roots in Denver and work in the home office."

At this point, Stavros sat up, propping himself with his arm. "You mean for good?"

"Yes. When we left Denver, he had everything put in storage. Furniture, photographs, albums, so many things I've never seen. Things I've forgotten that are mine. He plans to buy a house for us."

Stavros lay back on the lounger. "I wonder if a man can return home after so many years away and find the happiness he's looking for."

Andrea jumped out of the chair. Thoughts of that future without Stavros sounded so bleak, she could hardly stand it. "I've been haunted by the same question. Now you know why I don't like talking about it."

"I'm sorry, Andrea. It was insensitive of me."

"Not at all. I'm going to run inside and bring you the laptop. I plan itineraries for tours and am interested to see what you have mapped out for us."

When she came back to the patio, she found Stavros on the phone. She heard the name Theo and knew he was talking about business. How much he would divulge to his colleagues about his father's ploy, she didn't know. He hid his heartache well, but deep down she knew he had to be devastated.

After handing him the computer, she slipped inside the house for her novel, imagining he'd be on the phone for quite a while. She couldn't conceive of her father doing something so cruel. And even though Stavros's father might not carry through with his scheme, it didn't take away the hurt of betrayal.

When she came back out on the patio, she found he'd finished his conversation. His eyes were closed.

There were shadows and lines on his arresting face that hadn't been there before his brother had shown up last night. Alarmed, she cried, "Is your pain worse again?"

He turned his head toward her and opened his eyes. Through the black lashes they looked like a dark cloud before a storm. "It's not my leg."

"Then it's this threat your father poses."

"Afraid so. Theo and Zander will be arriving at the house within the hour so we can talk strategy."

"I'll make more iced tea and fix some sandwiches."

"Andrea Linford, do you know you're the best thing that ever happened to me?"

Stavros, Stavros. Don't say things like that. Don't you know I'm dying inside at the thought of leaving you?

CHAPTER SEVEN

MONDAY MORNING, STAVROS was able to walk out to the car on his own. Yesterday's rest had made all the difference. He stretched out in the backseat with his laptop and waited for Andrea to come. She was so practical she packed everything they'd both need in her duffel bag for their overnight trip. He loved it. His and her things all thrown together. A precursor of a future with her. He refused to think any other way.

Stavros watched her walk toward him dressed in a wraparound khaki skirt and a cream-colored knit top. Her shapely figure did wonders for anything she wore. The guys had done triple takes when he'd introduced them to Andrea yesterday. Theo was married, but Zander was still a bachelor and had had a hard time keeping his eyes to himself.

She'd brought them a never-ending supply of food and drinks. Stavros could tell how impressed they were that she knew so much about their line of work and had been inside the plant.

He'd asked her to stay with him while they discussed the threat facing them. His partners hadn't left until much later that evening because Andrea had entertained them with a few hair-raising stories of her adventures in the Gran Chaco of Paraguay. Close calls with a poison dart and a feeding frenzy of piranha fish in an area inhabited by natives who spoke Guarani had had them glued to every word. She'd fit in like a guy, but retained a beguiling femininity.

He heard her close the trunk, and then she came around and slid behind the wheel. She looked over her shoulder. "Have we remembered everything? Did you talk to Raisa?"

"I told her we wouldn't be back until Tuesday night."

"Then we're good to go." She started the engine and backed the car around. "I used to think it might be kind of fun being a driver for some top-brass military general. But driving the legendary Kyrie Konstantinos around is much better."

He never knew what was going to come out of her luscious mouth next. Their eyes met through the rearview mirror. Hers were a vibrant blue this morning.

"Why's that?"

"Because you're in a different kind of war—one I believe in—and I want you to win."

Sometimes the things Andrea said and the way she said them…

"Maybe my father won't fire the first shot after all."

"Maybe not. One lives in hope."

Yes, one does.

"Stavros? Why do you think he's the way he is? You know what I mean."

"Leon and I have asked each other that question dozens of times. Our grandfather, his own father, didn't understand him either. He always has to be right. I don't know where that comes from."

"Do your parents go to church?"

Her question made him want to laugh and cry at the same time, because she was trying to understand the complex relationship he had with his parents, which not even he could fix.

"On the important holidays. How about your father?"

"The same."

Stavros was curious. "Does he expect you to go?"

"Not anymore."

"What does that mean?"

"When we were living in Venezuela, I went to a Catholic school and a couple of nuns befriended me. For a while I thought I might like to be one when I grew older. When I told my dad, he had a fit."

"I'll bet."

"That was one of the few times I'd ever seen him really upset. He said he loved me so much he never wanted me to go away from him. At the time I believed him and gave up on the idea. But as I matured, I realized he really wanted me to grow up with the opportunity to be married and have children. He said children are a parent's greatest blessing."

"I know *you* are," Stavros said moodily.

"I've tried to be."

The trend in their conversation had become painful for him. Her father wanted his daughter to be married, but only on *his* terms? Father, daughter and son-in-law all under the same roof in Denver, Colorado?

"We've arrived at the first quarry on the list." She got out and came around to open his door. "I'll go inside and see if the manager will come out to talk to you. Wish me luck."

"There isn't enough money to pay what I owe you, Andrea."

"Don't be silly." She headed for the quarry office. He experienced pure pleasure just watching the womanly way she moved. Her hair shimmered in the sun.

He'd wanted to get a head start finding new sources of marble material, but feared this wouldn't work if he didn't make the initial introduction. The doctor had told him not to walk around on his bad leg until tomorrow. His wound was feeling better, so he'd be a fool not to follow his advice.

Soon, he saw Andrea accompanied by an older man. Stavros lowered his legs to the floor and got out so at least he was standing. They both joined him. She'd given the manager one of his business cards.

"When your beautiful assistant said Kyrie Stavros Konstantinos himself was outside waiting with a proposition for us, I couldn't believe it. You were stung by a stingray?"

"That's right. I still have trouble walking."

"You're lucky to still be alive. I could tell you stories."

Out of the corner of his eye, he could see Andrea smiling.

"Thankfully my story has a happy ending, otherwise I wouldn't be standing here, but it's all I can manage."

The quarry manager scratched his head. "This is a very unusual way to do business. You were very smart to send her first." His mouth widened into a grin. "So you are now in business for yourself. No more papa?"

Stavros had to smother a groan. "I still have a papa, but no more ties to the Konstantinos Corporation. My partners and I are in business producing a new product called Marma-Kon." He took advantage of the moment to explain why he wanted to buy their marble waste.

"I'll email you the contract today so you can read it over. It should answer all your questions. If you are in agreement to do business, contact Theo Troikas, whose name is on the card. He's the contracts manager."

"I tell you what. I have to talk to the owner. He owns two quarries. I think he will say yes, but I'll get back to you. Thank you, and get well." He shook Stavros's hand.

After he'd walked away, Stavros climbed in the backseat once more and Andrea closed the door for him. Then she got back in the driver's seat and turned around. "What do you think?"

Stavros stretched out to rest his leg. "Do you even have to ask? With you as my ambassador, it was like taking candy from a baby. The hitch will come when he talks to the owner."

"Why wouldn't he agree? They'll be making money off you."

"You never know. Prejudice maybe, because I'm the son who's no longer working for his father. The owner's a proud Greek, remember? We're a pretty patriarchal bunch."

She nodded. "With the god Zeus serving as the role model, you are. His autocratic handling of his son Arcas was a great example of fatherly love. That poor boy was so upset he said, 'If you think you're so clever, Father, make me whole and unharmed.' That relationship got nowhere in a hurry."

That was a little-known part of the myth. The fact that she could pull such information out of her head at a moment's notice astounded him.

"Stavros—" Her eyes clouded over. "I'm trying to get you to ease up on yourself. You're not actually buying into your own pathetic fiction about not living up to your father's expectations? As far as I'm concerned, you've exceeded any dreams a father might have for his son. The respect everyone has for you should warm your heart."

"Does it warm yours?" He couldn't see her face.

"I told you the other night that I've chosen to believe in you."

Stavros put his head back. "If only I'd heard that kind of faith come from my father, even one time…"

"Please don't torture yourself." She had tears in her voice. "You need to stop! Your brother, Leon, is your champion or he wouldn't have come to the house the other night to warn you. Even if you didn't notice it, I saw the manager's eyes gleam while you told him about your product. He stood there wishing he'd thought of it first and probably wished he had a son like you.

"You're really onto something big, Stavros. As long as you're searching for new sources, why not buy some quarries no longer being used? You know the old saying about one man's trash being another man's treasure."

"They cost money, but I hear what you're saying, Andrea." Every single brilliant word.

"Good. Then let's drive on to the next target."

Andrea marveled at the scenery after they reached the place where they were spending the night. Outside the door of her hotel room, which adjoined Stavros's, she looked south and east to the pine trees and sweet chestnut forests. They surrounded the village sitting at the foot of Mount Ypsarion. Its charm lay in the old houses with their stone walls and wooden roofs.

While he got ready for bed, she went to a local *taverna* for oven-baked pizza that was chewy like focaccia bread and topped with gyro meat in a sauce tasting strongly of basil. After she returned, they drank fruit juice in lieu of wine with their meal. Knowing Stavros had a sweet tooth, she'd picked up some baklava.

Before she got ready for bed, she went back to his room to make sure he'd taken his pills and was settled. She knew he was tired, but he seemed in better spirits than when they'd stopped at the first quarry.

She felt his eyes on her the second she entered his room. "How do you feel after meeting with managers from three different quarries?"

"I'll know better when contracts come in, but I'm satisfied we've made a dent."

"Do you think you're up to more visits tomorrow?"

"Are you?" he questioned right back. "You must be exhausted after all you've done today."

"I'm not the one with the wound. If you don't mind, I'd like to check it before you go to sleep, just to be on the safe side." She pulled a clean dressing from the box.

He threw the covers aside. For his convenience, obviously, he'd put on a pair of shorts for bed. Nothing else. The dusting of black hair on his well-defined chest reminded her of those hours on the beach when they'd gotten tangled in each other's arms. As if reading her mind, he turned over. She sucked in her breath and leaned down to make an inspection.

Relief swept through her. "It's healing, Stavros. There's almost no drainage."

"That means I can do my own walking tomorrow."

"Within reason," she reminded him. After discarding the old dressing, she washed her hands and came out of the bathroom to affix a new one. "Is there anything else I can do for you?"

"Stay with me tonight, Andrea," he asked in a compelling voice. "Lie by me."

"Stavros—"

"I swear I won't do anything you don't want me to do. We don't have a lot of time left before you're gone for good."

She knew that a lot better than he did. She'd had nightmares about never seeing him again. But what he was asking would be a mistake for both of them, a voice inside warned. Stavros had no idea how much she'd come to love him. To spend more time with him was only going to make it harder to leave. After losing Ferrante, she was terrified of loving another man again.

"Can't we at least have this night together like we had out in the woods when we were looking for Darren? I don't know about you, but I remember every moment of it lying next to you. I remember your fragrance. You always smell divine, did you know that?"

Andrea could hardly breathe. "Let me think about it." She darted toward the door that separated their two rooms. Once inside hers, she reached in the duffel bag for her nightgown and robe. During her shower, her brain screamed at her to remain in her room until morning. But by the time she'd brushed her teeth and was ready for bed, her heart had won out. Stavros was right. This would be their last night together before she had to fly back to Thessaloniki.

On legs that trembled, she turned off the light and went into his bedroom. His light was off too. She drifted through the semidarkness to the bed. Without removing her robe, she got in on the other side. No sooner had she rested her head on the pillow than she felt his arm snake around her waist and roll her into his strong body.

"Finally," he said in an unsteady voice and buried his face in her hair. "I've been willing you to come to me. I love you, *agape mou*." His hand roved over her arm and back possessively. "I fell in love with you that day on the mountain. I'm a different man because of it. Don't tell me it's too soon to say those words to you."

Tears trickled out of her eyes. "I won't. I love you too. But you already know that, in the same way you know everything else," she murmured against his lips. "I adore you." She kissed him over and over again. "I knew it when you got out of your car to castigate me for losing one of my students."

"Forgive me, darling."

"There's nothing to forgive. I didn't think a man like you existed, yet there you were, bigger than life and so handsome I didn't think my heart could take it.

When I thought I might never see you again, I asked if I could look for Darren with you. It was so bold of me I should be ashamed, but I couldn't help myself."

"Do you think a lesser woman could ever hold me?" Stavros kissed her long and hard before he lifted his head. She moaned in protest. "We need to talk, my love. About us."

"Let's not ruin tonight with talk," she begged.

"There are other ways of communicating." He covered her face with kisses. "It's all I can do to keep myself from making love to you, but I made you a promise."

She loved him more fiercely for honoring it. Once again, she was the one spinning out of control. This wasn't fair to him.

"If I stay in this bed any longer, then I'll pay a price for giving in to my desire. It'll be too heavy a price considering I'll be gone soon. It's already tearing me apart to imagine leaving you. But my agony will never end if I sleep with you tonight. After knowing your possession, nothing will ever be the same for me again. I know myself too well."

Stavros propped his head on his hand to look at her. "You're talking about Ferrante."

"No. When Ferrante found out I'd never been intimate with a man, he said he wanted me to be his wife before he took me to bed. I loved him for loving me that much. For several months after his death, I was angry because I felt I'd been cheated and it was my own fault.

"But because I didn't have that memory, I'm convinced it helped me to heal. Otherwise, how can I explain falling in love with *you* so fast? After meeting you, I can't imagine loving another man again whether we sleep together or not."

He smoothed some hair off her forehead. "So what are we going to do about us? Does your father expect you to stay with him for always?"

"It isn't a case of expect, Stavros. I'm the one who doesn't want him to be alone."

"Why? It's normal for a grown woman to fall in love with a man and set up her own household."

She buried her face in his neck. "I know, but— Oh, you just don't understand."

"Try me. Please."

"He's so selfless and has never asked for anything for himself. I can't bear to think of him alone to live out the rest of his life. His parents were killed in a train accident when he was young. He had to live with an aunt, but she died before he met Mom. Then she died giving birth to me. I'm all he has left in this world."

The words came out in heavy sobs. Stavros held her closer, kissing her hair and cheek. Ferrante had loved her enough to know what he had to do to keep her. Maybe there was another way around what seemed to be an insoluble problem, because Stavros flat-out refused to lose her.

When the sobs subsided, Andrea rolled away from him and stood up, realizing she'd taken him by surprise. "I've given you all the honesty I have in me, but now I know what I have to do. I'd only be torturing myself to stay the rest of the night with you. Our meeting at the quarry was accidental. We've had some very precious moments together, but we need to get on with our lives since they're going in different directions. Try to get some sleep. We have two more quarries to visit tomorrow."

Andrea hurried to bed. She tossed and turned most of the night. After awakening early, she dressed and slipped out to bring breakfast back. She avoided Stavros's eyes as she put their food on the table in his room and reached for a roll. He'd dressed in white lightweight trousers and a collared tan shirt. He looked terrific and could walk a lot better this morning.

After eating, she packed up the duffel bag and turned to him. "Have you taken your medicine?"

He reached for his coffee. "I took it when I got out of bed. Thank you for the reminder and the food."

"You're welcome. I'll just take this bag out to the car and wait for you."

"I'll be right there."

In another few minutes, he climbed into the passenger seat next to her and they drove away.

"Are you sure you wouldn't be more comfortable in back?" After driving around in the Jeep with him, it was a strange experience with him sitting next to her in his elegant car. She was so aware of him, it was hard to concentrate.

"I'm fine. But after we've stopped at the next quarry, I want to go back to the house. I've decided I can accomplish much the same thing by making phone calls from home."

She frowned. "Do you wish you hadn't come?"

"No. It was necessary for me to see if my physical presence has made a difference. But in every case, the person I really need to convince isn't on the premises.

Part of the reason I wanted to do things this way was so I could spend more time alone with you."

She'd loved this time with him more than he would ever know.

"However, since I don't need any more help, and because being together has put an unbearable strain on both of us, I'll let you get back to your office. The helicopter will be waiting to take you. I daresay your boss will be thrilled to see you walk in."

Andrea's heart plunged to her feet. Stavros admitted he'd fallen in love with her, but sometime between last night and this morning, he'd had some sort of epiphany. She knew what he was like. Once he'd made up his mind, that was it. He'd made a decision about the two of them, the only one that made sense.

There was no going back to the way they had been before last night and they both knew it. But she was so devastated it took all her strength to focus while negotiating the mountain roads. Stavros worked on his laptop, not interested in talking to her. They'd run out of words. He was able to freeze her out, an ability she'd give anything to possess.

By noon they'd visited the quarry before heading back toward Panagia. She had no idea if he'd felt it was a successful morning or not. En route, they stopped for food, which they ate in the car. He turned on some typical soft rock music, his way of letting her know the music wouldn't bother him while he did work on his computer.

They arrived at his villa just after two o'clock. His fabulous house felt more like home to her than any furnished apartment she and her dad had ever lived in over the years. Her heart was in so much pain, she wondered if it could literally break.

Andrea let Stavros off in front. Even if he was walking better, he shouldn't have to climb a lot of steps yet. After he shut the door, she drove around to the back and parked the car next to the Jeep. His posh Mercedes had been a sheer pleasure to drive. When she let herself in the back door, she found he'd gone straight to his den.

Taking advantage of the time, she went to his bedroom and unpacked the duffel bag. Toiletries in the bathroom, medicine on his side table. As for her own packing, there was very little to do. In ten minutes, she was ready to go. The sooner, the better, because she was on the verge of breaking down.

On her way to the kitchen with her bag, the front doorbell rang. Maybe Raisa had come to the house for some reason, but didn't want to just walk in on them. Since Stavros was still in the den, she walked through the alcove to the door and opened it.

A stern-faced man in some kind of uniform handed her an express mail envelope. "Are you Andrea Linford?"

"Yes?"

"This is for you and Kyrie Konstantinos. See that he gets it."

What on earth? She watched him go down the steps before she shut the door.

Stavros was right behind her as she turned around. He caught her in his arms. For a moment, she saw the torment in his eyes. It matched her own.

His fingers kneaded her skin before he released her with seeming reluctance. "Who was that?"

"A—a courier," she stammered and handed him the envelope.

He ripped it open and pulled out an official-looking document. She watched him as he read it and saw lines of anger mar his striking features. For the first time since she'd known him, she heard him let go a curse.

Andrea got a sick feeling in the pit of her stomach. "Stavros? What is it?"

His eyes went hard as flint when he looked at her. "Draco Nasso is suing me for breach of promise to his pregnant daughter Christina and naming *you* co-respondent. We're both to appear before the judge day after tomorrow in Kavala."

She shook her blond head. "You didn't promise her anything! He has no just cause!"

"That doesn't matter to him," he said in a gravelly voice. "He most likely owns the judge in question. Come in the den with me while we get my attorney on the phone. Everything's coming into play even faster than I had thought." His gaze shot to hers. "With Draco on the warpath, my father's threat will be realized. Thank providence you were here to help me get around to those quarries."

This couldn't be happening, but it was. "While you do that, I'll be happy to call the quarries we didn't get to visit on the mainland and set up conferences on Skype for you."

She heard him inhale sharply. "How did I ever function without you?"

How am I going to live without you, Stavros?

They walked to the den. "Go ahead and sit at my

desk. The file is open with all the phone numbers. Call the ones that don't have a check by them."

Andrea was thankful to be able to help and got busy making the calls. Stavros sat in one of the chairs near his bookcase and got on the phone with his attorney. He was still on the phone when she'd finished lining up appointments.

"Andrea?" He covered the mouthpiece of his phone. "Since you're sitting in front of the screen, would you be willing to speak with my attorney over Skype now? He can take your deposition this way and present it in court without you having to be present."

"I'll do anything you ask."

His eyes thanked her before he spoke to his attorney once more. In another minute, they rang off. Stavros walked over and set everything up. His hands slid to her shoulders from behind. He squeezed them gently.

"I know how horrendous this is for you," he said in a low voice near her ear.

"It's you I'm worried about," she murmured shakily.

"It's another form of harassment to wear me down, but it'll be over soon. My attorney's name is Myron Karras."

Within seconds, Mr. Karras appeared before her. "I can see you just fine, Despinis Linford."

"I can see you too, Kyrie Karras."

"Fine. We'll do this in a question-and-answer format. If you're ready, we'll start now."

She eyed Stavros. "I'm ready."

"Please state your full name, nationality, age, marital status, address and occupation please."

Andrea complied.

"When was the first time you met Stavros Konstantinos."

"At quarry three on Thassos Island." She named the date and time.

"Why did *you* specifically come to the quarry?" After she'd explained, he said, "When the teen wasn't found, what did you do?"

Her cheeks went hot. Stavros had sat down on another chair, studying her through veiled eyes.

"Though the police had started a search for him, Kyrie Konstantinos said he was going to go look for Darren because he knew the mountain well and felt somewhat responsible."

"Why would he say that?"

"Because he was the one who gave permission through the quarry manager to let our tour groups come to the quarry. I asked if I could go with him because I'm the one who planned the student-teacher tour to the quarry in the first place and also felt partially responsible."

"Did you two go alone?"

She shivered. "Yes. I followed him to his villa, where I left my rental car. He packed a hamper of food and we left in his Jeep. We were out all night looking for him and eventually found Darren hiding in a truck on the morning ferry ready to leave Thassos for Keramoti. The police lieutenant in charge of the case took Darren into custody."

"What did you do then?"

"Kyrie Konstantinos drove us back to his villa, where I got into my rental car and left for Thessaloniki."

"Why did you arrange for tours to go to that particular quarry?"

"My father, Paul Linford, took me to quarry three when we first arrived in Greece. He said it produced the whitest marble of all. I thought it should be added to the tour agenda and made arrangements through the quarry manager, Gus…"

"Patras," Stavros whispered.

"Gus Patras. He got permission from the Konstantinos Corporation to allow tour groups to visit."

"Before you were hired by PanHellenic Tours, where did you live?"

"Italy."

"Before that?"

"Venezuela, and before that French Guiana, Paraguay and India." She rattled it all off to get it over with.

The attorney's brows lifted at that bit of information, producing a half smile from Stavros.

"So you'd never been in Greece before."

She and Stavros exchanged a silent glance. They both knew where these questions were leading. "Never. Because of my father's work, we were sent to Greece and got an apartment in Thessaloniki. I went to the university there, then was hired by PanHellenic Tours."

"Who hired you?"

"Sakis Manos, the owner."

"How did you happen to go to Thassos Island at all?"

"My father is a chemical engineer, interested in the history and geology of Greece. Thassos fascinated him because he said it was a big lump of marble."

"What else can you tell me about him?"

"He works for W.B. Smythe, an American engineering company based in Denver, Colorado, where I was born." After explaining his job, she said, "We traveled around when he had time off. He told me the marble quarries had existed anciently and I should visit them. Since he's the smartest man I've ever known, I was eager to see them."

Stavros's attorney smiled. "To your knowledge, did your father ever meet Kyrie Konstantinos or talk to him?"

"No."

"Tell me the date, time and circumstances involving you and Kyrie Konstantinos that prompted the 911 call."

No wonder Stavros had told her she shouldn't have mentioned his name to the dispatcher. The news traveled so fast, it had reached the ears of Tina's father in no time. She explained everything the best she could.

"So you were there to take him home and nurse him."

"Yes. His stingray wound needed watching."

"When did you first meet Christina Nasso?"

Oh, no. Andrea mentioned the date and time.

"What were the circumstances?"

"I was in his house when she came to visit him unexpectedly."

"Did you see her?"

"Yes. In the front hall."

"Did you hear anything?"

She darted Stavros a nervous glance. "Yes. She came to talk to him about her pregnancy. He denied being the father and asked her to leave."

"Are you involved with him?"

Blood hammered in her ears. "We've spent a little time together, but I'll be in Brazil in a few more days with my father, where he has work."

"You're resigning your job with PanHellenic Tours?"

"Yes."

"Are you leaving because you believe Kyrie Konstantinos is the father of the baby and you have no hope of marrying him for his money?"

"No!" Enraged by the question, she shot out of the chair, then realized where she was and sat down again. "I have no hope of anything!" Not without Stavros.

"I'm leaving because my father loves and needs me. As for Kyrie Konstantinos, he told me he has never loved her and ended their brief relationship over three months ago. I believe him. Besides my father, he's the most honorable man I've ever known."

"Is there anything else you'd like to add or change to your testimony?"

"No."

"Thank you."

The screen went blank, but Andrea didn't notice because she'd already hidden her wet face in her hands.

CHAPTER EIGHT

I HAVE NO hope of anything!

Andrea's plaintive cry resounded in Stavros's heart. He turned off the computer before pulling her into his arms. For a long time, he simply rocked her back and forth in an effort to give her comfort while he drew some solace from simply holding her. Those quiet little sobs shook him to the deepest recesses of his soul.

He kissed her forehead. "You didn't deserve any of this. I know that deposition was brutal, but Myron had to learn everything he could so he'll be prepared when he and I go before the judge. If Tina is pregnant, it's not mine. When a DNA test is done, then she'll have to come clean. If she isn't pregnant, she'll be cited for contempt.

"At that point my attorney will bring a lawsuit for perjury. In the end, her father will be the all-time loser, but I know that doesn't repair the damage this has done to you." He kissed her eyes and cheeks. "There's no way to make this up to you, Andrea. Ask me for anything. If it's within my power to give, I'll do it."

She sniffed and lifted her head. She looked at him

through glazed eyes. "I know you would. What I need is to get back to Thessaloniki. Is your pilot down on the pad?"

His pain was worse than any the stingray had inflicted. "Yes."

"Then I'd like to leave now."

A great shudder racked his body before he released her and reached for his phone on the computer desk. He called the pilot and told him to get ready for takeoff. After he hung up, his gaze darted to hers. "Do you have everything packed?"

"Yes."

With a sense of inevitability, Stavros picked up the duffel bag against her protest. Her nursing days were over. They walked through the house and down the back steps to the pad. When they reached it, he cupped her face in his hands and kissed her precious mouth one more time before helping her into the helicopter. Anything more and he wouldn't have been able to let her go.

"You'll be home before dark. There'll be a limo at the heliport waiting to drive you to your apartment."

She wore a pained expression. "You don't have to do that."

"After what you've lived through and sacrificed for me, you can say that? I want to give you everything. I'm the one who absconded with you on Friday after work and brought you into this hornet's nest. The least I can do is make certain you get home safely."

He could tell she was struggling to swallow. "Thank you for everything, Stavros. I'll never forget." Her voice trembled.

No. Stavros wouldn't forget either.

He shut the door and stepped away. The rotors started up and began to whine. He waved to her as the helicopter lifted off and swung in a northwesterly direction toward Thessaloniki.

Last night, their passion for each other had driven them over a threshold to a more precarious place. He knew it had shaken her. Though she'd professed her love for him, they were in an impossible situation because the bond with her father went fathoms deep.

Without a mother all her life, Andrea revered the man who'd raised her. She was so attached to her father, she wouldn't allow another man to come between them if it meant a separation.

I'm leaving because my father loves and needs me.

That said it all. Stavros didn't blame Andrea for anything, but he refused to pressure her. His parents had done that to him his whole life and it had caused a rift he doubted could ever be mended. Look what pressure had done to Tina.

Andrea would have to come to terms with her emotions on her own. Ferrante had recognized he wanted her enough to accommodate her. But Stavros didn't have that luxury. He'd started a new business. Hundreds of plant workers and truck drivers depended on him. If he wanted her with him, he would have to find a way, but there were certain things he needed to clear up first.

Stavros had achieved two of his lifelong dreams, but the third one still eluded him. To find the right woman was difficult enough, but to make a relationship work meant sacrifice on both parts to achieve real happiness.

When he couldn't see the helicopter any longer, he walked back in the house and headed for his den. His work was never ending. That was good because he doubted he'd be able to sleep. For the time being, Andrea was only as far away as Thessaloniki, but she might as well be on another planet.

After his flight to Kavala on Thursday for the hearing generated by evil design, he'd fly to Thessaloniki and see her one last time. He couldn't leave her hanging about the results of the hearing. She deserved to know the outcome from him in person. If he went to her office before she left work, she couldn't refuse to see him.

Once seated at his desk, he opened the accounts file. The difference between profit and loss was in the numbers, which he constantly scrutinized for errors. While he was deep in calculations, his cell phone rang. It couldn't be Andrea. She was still in the air, but just the thought of her caused his pulse to speed up.

He checked the caller ID and clicked on. "Leon?"

"Hey, bro. I heard old man Nasso served you with a breach of promise notice."

"He did more than that. He named Andrea codefendant."

"He's a sick man. Does Andrea know?"

"She was the one served when she answered my door."

"Hell, Stav."

"There's more. Myron deposed her on a Skype conference call so she won't have to appear at the hearing. The questions tore her apart. Right now she's flying home in the helicopter. In another few days, she'll be going to Brazil with her father."

"I thought you loved her."

His eyes closed tightly. "With every fiber of my being."

"Then how come she's leaving?" When Stavros didn't answer, his brother called, "Stav?"

"I'm still here."

"Does she know you love her?"

"Yes."

"Does she love you?"

"Yes."

"Then what in the hell is the problem?"

"Because she's leaving with her father, and my life is here."

"You're serious."

"Afraid so." Stavros told his brother about Ferrante. "He gave up everything for her. It was the only way he could have her."

Leon was quiet for a long time. "That's a tough one. I don't envy what you're going through. I wish there was something I could do to help."

"Just be in my corner like you've always been."

"Stav—I don't like the idea of you being in your hideaway all alone. Why don't you come to my house and stay with us and the kids. I'll go with you when it's time to see the judge."

"Thanks for the offer, but I'm not fit company for anyone."

"If you need me, call anytime, day or night. I mean that."

"I know. Talk to you soon."

The depression he'd lived with before Andrea had come into his life had descended on him like a paralyzing, impenetrable darkness.

Andrea had been home from work for only a few minutes on Wednesday evening when she heard a knock on the apartment door.

"Andrea?" a familiar voice called out.

"Dad!" She couldn't believe he was here.

He opened the door with his own key. "Hi, honey. I decided to surprise you."

She flew into his arms and hugged him so hard, he laughed. "What's going on?" When she lifted her tearstained face, he frowned. "I thought you were happy to see me, but you look like the Wreck of the Hesperus."

That was a playful expression of her father's he often used to make her laugh when she was upset. But she was in too much pain since leaving Stavros to respond.

He wiped the moisture from her cheeks. "Hey— this *is* serious. It's a good thing I was able to finish up my work early and get home to you."

"Do you mean you're through at the mine? Literally?"

"Yes, honey. I told my superior I needed to help my daughter get ready for our move to Brazil." There was more gray in his dark blond hair, but she hadn't noticed until he cocked his head. "How come I've walked in to find you in tears? Is this still about Ferrante?"

She shook her head.

"Do you enjoy your job so much it's going to be hard to leave?"

"That's not it, Dad, although I'll miss Sakis."

"Okay. I'll stop playing twenty questions. For you to be in this kind of shape, your problem has to do with a man."

"Yes."

"He wouldn't by any chance be the mastermind behind that plant, would he?"

"Yes."

Her father was so smart he could always divine what was wrong with her. "Those pictures you sent were pretty impressive. Come on. Out with it." He put his arm around her shoulders and walked her over to the couch. Then he sat down in the chair near the coffee table.

"I don't know where to start."

He leaned forward. "The beginning is always a good place. What's his name?"

"Stavros Konstantinos."

"You're talking the Konstantinos Marble Corporation, of course."

"That's the one, except that he no longer works for the family. He has started his own company." Her father had opened the floodgate and it all came spilling out. Everything about the time she'd spent with him, the search for Darren, the problems with his parents, the hearing before the judge because she had been named codefendant.

"Unfortunately, having a name like Konstantinos and all the money that goes with it makes him a living target. Has he asked you to marry him, honey?"

"No." Her voice shook. "He knows I'm leaving Greece with you." She got up from the couch, unable to sit still.

"Does he know about Ferrante?"

"Everything."

"Have you told Stavros you're dying of love for him?"

"Yes."

"Then why are you going to Brazil with me?"

She wheeled around to stare at her father. "Because I love you and don't want you to be alone."

He got a troubled look on his face. "Did you tell *him* that?"

"Yes. What's wrong?"

Her father stood up. "Honey—I hope you're not sacrificing your own happiness because you're worried about me."

"Of course I'm worried about you. We've never been apart."

"I'm afraid that's my fault. I think I've done a terrible thing to you without realizing it."

"What do you mean?"

"Somewhere along the way you've decided you have to be my caretaker."

"No, Dad. It's not like that."

"It's exactly like that," he countered. "So *that's* why Ferrante was willing to move around with us. I thought it odd, but you seemed so happy about it, I never questioned it."

She was shocked. "Dad—"

"Honey, this is the last thing I ever wanted to happen. I raised you hoping that one day you'd get married. It broke my heart when Ferrante was killed. Now that you've met another wonderful man, I don't want to be the reason why you don't stay here and really get to know Stavros. You've known each other,

what? All of two weeks? You need more time together."

She couldn't believe he was saying these things.
"But what will you do?"

"Without you?" He laughed. "I have my own life
to lead, but we'll always have each other. If you love
this man heart and soul, then you need to stay here
and give it a chance. I'd give anything if your mother
were here right now. If she were alive, she'd give you
the same advice. Honey—you and I will get together
whenever possible, right? But you need to pursue your
own life."

Andrea had never loved her father more than at
this moment. "Yes! Oh, yes!"

He held out his arms and she ran into them. The
tears kept coming. Just a different kind. "I want you
to meet him. He's so wonderful, you can't imagine."

"I think I got a clue when you sent me those pictures. Now how about showing me a picture of him?"

"I will, but first you need to know he's in trouble and I've been named codefendant because of that
woman."

"They mean business, don't they?"

"I'm afraid so." For the next little while, she told
him everything. "His father has never shown him
love."

"Some people don't know how, but he had to have
loved him all these years, otherwise why would he
let his son be the managing director of the corporation?"

She blinked. "You're right!" Her dad could always
make her feel better. "But I can hardly stand how
much he's been hurt. When you meet Stavros, you

just won't believe how fantastic he is. For this woman's father to put pressure on Stavros's father and take him to court just tears me apart."

"Sounds like this woman's father would do anything to have Stavros for a son-in-law."

"He tried because Stavros is a breed apart from other men. But Stavros doesn't see himself as exceptional."

"Maybe it'll be up to you to help him take off the blinders. Anyway, nothing at this hearing is going to stick. He says it's not his baby, so at some point it's all going to come out in the wash one way or another. I've been there and know it for a fact."

She smiled up at him. "Your facts outweigh everyone else's. You've always been the smartest man I've ever known."

"You mean until you collided with Stavros Konstantinos."

"If you hadn't taken me to Thassos to visit the marble quarry, we would never have met."

Elek Cadmus, the attorney for Draco Nasso, was known for his cutthroat tactics. Stavros didn't put anything past him. There were five of them in the judge's courtroom for the closed hearing Myron had insisted upon. But he couldn't prevent Tina from being present.

When Stavros saw her and her father sitting by the attorney, he thought she looked pale. Maybe she *was* pregnant and had morning sickness.

They'd already heard the recording of Andrea's deposition. Now the judge addressed Myron. "We want to hear about the events of the evening when your client and Despinis Linford began their search for the missing teen known as Darren Lewis."

Myron stood up. "The court has heard her deposition. My client has nothing more to add."

"I'd like more details, Your Honor," Elek demanded.

The judge nodded to Stavros. There was no question the judge was in Draco's pocket to allow this farce to continue.

"We left in my Jeep for the Dragon Cave near Panagia, thinking we might find the teen hiding there. After staying inside for a half hour without seeing him, we left and drove through the forest looking for him. Finally we stopped and camped out, sleeping separately—she in a bedroll, I on some blankets."

"Did you and Despinis Linford have physical contact? Remember, you're under oath."

"No, we did not. At dawn, we went into Panagia for breakfast and asked salespeople in several bike shops if they'd seen the young American. When nothing panned out, we drove down to the ferry landing and went aboard thinking he might be hiding in one of the cars or trucks. We found him hiding under the tarp of a truck. After the police came for him, I drove us back to my home. She left in the helicopter."

"I've already listened to your mother's deposition. In it, she states that when she arrived at your villa, she discovered you and Despinis Linford were having lunch on your patio after having spent the night together."

"That's correct, but my guest slept in the guest bedroom."

"Why did you invite her?"

"Because I was attracted to her and wanted to spend more time with her."

"You were taken to a clinic by ambulance due to a sting from a stingray. It was Despinis Linford who called 911. By this time, were the two of you lovers?"

His hands tightened into fists. "No."

"Do you deny she stayed overnight after you came home from the hospital?"

"No. She nursed me while I was confined to my bed. She saved my life and I'll always be in her debt."

"Do you still deny you're the father of Christina Nasso's baby?"

"Yes." For the second time during the hearing, Stavros looked at Tina and her glowering father. "We were never lovers and I never made a promise to marry her. A DNA test will be the proof."

Elek looked at the judge. "I have no more questions, Your Honor."

"Very well. I've heard all the testimony I need. This case will stay open until a DNA test can be made after the baby is born to determine paternity. At that time, I'll deliver a verdict."

He addressed Myron. "Neither of your clients is free to leave the country until my verdict is rendered. This hearing is adjourned until further notice."

Andrea couldn't leave?

Stavros was too jubilant to sit still. After the judge vacated the room, he turned to Myron. "Thank you for all you've done."

"You're welcome, but it was a waste of time."

"No, it wasn't." The judge's ruling would keep Andrea close to him.

"What do you mean?"

"I'll explain later. It's clear Draco wanted to punish me. Now that he's had the chance, I want to forget about it."

"If you get any more harassment, call me immediately."

"Of course."

"Can I give you a lift to Thessaloniki in my car?"

"No, thanks. My driver is waiting outside to take me to the heliport. First though, I need to phone Andrea. She needs to know today's outcome." *I have to tell her she must stay in Greece under a court order.*

They shook hands and Myron left, leaving Stavros alone in the courtroom. No sooner had he pulled out his cell phone than he thought he heard the door open. He turned his head to discover Tina hurrying toward him. Her father was nowhere in sight. As she drew closer, he could see she'd been crying.

She put out a hand. "Please, Stavros. I'm not here to cause you more trouble. My father thinks I'm in the restroom and he's waiting for me in the limo. I don't blame you if you hate me forever.

"The truth is, I'm not pregnant, but my parents think I am. When I get home I'm going to tell them I made it up because I didn't want to lose you. If my father doesn't tell your parents the truth and call off this lawsuit, then I will. That's all I have to say except I'm sorry I put you and Despinis Linford through this. What you told me at your house brought me to my senses. You were right. I can't let my parents' expectations drive my life anymore."

Stavros got out of the chair and hugged her. "We've both had to learn that lesson the hard way. Your truth has set both of us free. Good luck to you, Tina."

"You too, Stavros."

He phoned Myron immediately and told him what had just transpired. Myron said he'd get in touch with the other attorney to put a stop to the case. He doubted Tina would suffer from contempt of court since it was her father who'd engineered it.

Two hours later, Stavros rushed inside the building in Thessaloniki where Andrea worked. He wanted to deliver this news in person. But when he approached the receptionist at PanHellenic Tours, she told him Andrea had quit her job and wouldn't be coming back. He asked to speak to Sakis but learned the owner of the company was out of the office on business.

Something twisted in his gut. Was she still at her apartment packing, or had she gone without saying a final goodbye to him? She wouldn't do that to him, would she? He had to find out and took a taxi to her address.

No one answered the door. At this point, he tried her phone again, but all his calls went to her voice mail. Wherever she'd gone, she didn't want to be found. That was obvious. He didn't know where to turn. Frantic at this point, he left for the heliport to take the helicopter back to Thassos.

Once he reached the house, the emptiness of his life loomed so large it was unbearable. He couldn't stay there. As soon as he changed into jeans and a sport shirt, he got in the Jeep and drove to his office. There was a ton of work for him to catch up on while he waited for her to return his phone call.

Theo's car was still out in front. Another car was parked next to it. He didn't recognize it, but it didn't matter. After unlocking the main door with the remote, he headed for Theo's office, but as he passed his own, he noticed the door was open. He always kept it locked. Who'd been in there? And why?

"Stavros?"

He'd know that feminine voice anywhere and spun around in shock. There was Andrea, sitting in his desk chair looking sensational in a yellow sundress he'd never seen. She had an uncertain expression on her beautiful face, as if she didn't know what to expect from him.

"I've been waiting several hours for you. When you weren't at the villa, I didn't know what to do but come here. I hoped one of your partners could tell me where you were."

Stavros was afraid he was hallucinating. "How did you get here?"

"My dad's car. Theo let me in." She got to her feet. "Was the hearing ghastly?"

The hearing…he'd already forgotten about it. "Draco's attorney managed to make it as hideous as possible. When he'd finished my interrogation, the judge said he'd give his verdict after Tina's baby was born and the DNA results were in."

"Was she there?"

"Yes."

She bit her lip. "How horrible for you. I should have been there to support you."

"Andrea—Tina approached me after it was over. She admitted that she'd lied about the baby in order to hold on to me."

"Oh, Stavros—" The happiness in her voice was something he'd never forget.

"You believed in me. That was the support I

needed to get me through. She's going to tell both sets of parents. The lawsuit will be dropped. We made our peace."

Her eyes shimmered with tears. "How's your leg?"

"It's fine."

"That's good."

He couldn't take much more of this. "When are you and your father leaving?"

"Dad's already gone."

His heart lurched. "I don't understand."

"He finished up at the mine and now he's on his way to Brazil."

"But when I stopped by your office earlier, the receptionist told me you'd resigned and wouldn't be coming back. Why didn't you leave with your father?"

"I decided I'd rather stay here."

The blood pounded in his ears. "Why?"

"I'm tired of the tour business and would love to get a job working in an office or in a plant. You wouldn't happen to have a job opening for me, would you? Maybe a chauffeur? I'm not particular. I thought I'd rent an apartment in Panagia. It's my favorite village. Since Dad left the car with me, I have transportation now."

Stavros didn't know her in this mood. "Andrea— enough of your teasing. Why are you here?"

She moved closer to him. "You mean you really don't know?"

"If I did, I wouldn't be asking."

"I want to be near you. I love you until it hurts, but you already know that."

He did know. "But your father—you idolize him."

"That will never change, but another great love

has come into my life. There's room for both." She smiled that beautiful smile.

Stavros couldn't swallow. "I want you more than anything else in my life."

"But in what capacity?"

"In all the ways you can think of," he exploded.

"You mean like employee, friend, girlfriend, lover, confidante, nurse, cook, housekeeper? What?"

"I mean *wife*." The beautiful word reverberated against the walls of his office.

"I'd give anything to be your wife. Are you asking me?"

"Andrea—" His voice shook. "You've worked this out with him?"

She lounged against the edge of his desk. "We had a heart-to-heart the other day. He says he's lived the life he wants. Now he wants me to live the life I want. He says if I'm happy, then he won't worry about me and we'll always work things out to be together when we can. And in between times, we'll talk over Skype."

Stavros was incredulous.

"I think he feels like Tevye from *Fiddler on the Roof*, who wanted peace in his life, but in order to achieve it, he had to marry off his daughters first. Dad will go on leading his own life and wants me to lead mine. I believe him. He's going to be back in a month to see how I'm doing before he flies to Denver. Naturally he's anxious to meet you. I told him you're the smartest man I know next to him. That really got him going."

"You're being serious now."

Andrea could see her darling Stavros still needed

confirmation. She walked up to him and put her arms around his neck. "Life-and-death serious." Her voice throbbed. "After everything we've been through, do you really think I could leave you? Dad saw what a wreck I was the minute he walked in our apartment. He knew his daughter had lost her heart to another man. A great man. That's you."

Stavros could feel himself coming back to life.

"He was so sweet about it, Stavros. He said that two weeks wasn't nearly long enough for two people who've fallen madly in love to be torn apart. We need time to find out all the wonderful things that are still waiting for us. So I have an idea. Why don't we take a moonlight ride in the Jeep? There's this beautiful church in Panagia I want to show you."

"I'm way ahead of you, but before we do anything else, I want to do *this*." He wrapped her in his powerful arms and covered her mouth with his own. The urgency of his possessive kiss sent thrill after thrill through her body.

"I love you, Andrea. I love you. Don't ever leave me." He covered her face and throat with kisses.

"Stavros—don't you know by now I worship the ground you walk on."

"Knock, knock," sounded a male voice. "If this is a private party, I don't apologize because I'm too happy for you."

Stavros lifted his head, smiling broadly. "Theo— you're the first person to know Andrea and I are going to be married in a month." He sounded exultant, just the way she felt.

"Congratulations! Zander and I have had a bet on to see how long it would take you to propose.

He thought it might be another week, but I figured sooner. I won, but then I'm a married man and know the look of a man under the spell of woman magic."

"My wife-to-be has it in spades."

CHAPTER NINE

"Ready, honey?"

"I've been ready for this a long time." Andrea stood there outfitted in white silk, carrying gardenias. A lace mantilla covered her hair.

"You look like your mom did on our wedding day. Absolutely gorgeous."

"You're going to make me cry, Dad."

"We can't have that. Stavros is waiting for you at the front of the church. I like him, honey."

"I love him so much."

She put her hand on his arm, proud of her attractive father as they walked down the aisle of the Virgin Mary Church in Panagia. Her eyes fastened on Stavros. He looked so dark and splendid in his black dress suit, she couldn't see anyone else. But she knew the whole Konstantinos family and all of their close friends were there, with the exception of Stavros's father. Stavros didn't have hope that he'd come, but Andrea prayed he would.

Stavros had talked to the priest, expressing his desire that they have a simple ceremony. Over the past month Andrea had come to know him better and recognized his need for understatement, even in his religious vows. He truly was a modest man.

Her father led her to the front of the church and took her bouquet. Stavros reached for her hand and squeezed it. His gray eyes had a glow she'd never seen before. It ignited the flame that burned inside her. This was no longer a fairy tale, but blissful reality.

The priest nodded to them. "Andrea and Stavros, let us pray."

Their ceremony didn't take long. Rings were exchanged. She was so excited to be married to him, she could hardly wait for the part to come where the priest pronounced them husband and wife.

The second the words were spoken, Stavros drew her into his arms. "You could have no idea how long I've dreamed of this moment," he whispered against her lips before kissing her. For a little while, she forgot the world and kissed him back, unable to believe he was now her husband.

"Come on, you two," Leon murmured. "You're taking forever. Dad wants to be the first to congratulate you. He and Mom are waiting."

They both heard what Leon said. Andrea stopped kissing her husband. "Your father came," she whispered against his lips. Joy filled her heart. "Oh, darling—"

Stavros lifted his head. In that instant, she saw a light in those beautiful gray eyes she'd never seen before.

"I can see him. Except for silver in his hair, he's a cross between you and Leon."

Her husband crushed her to him. She knew what this moment meant to him. When he'd gotten hold of his emotions, he grasped her hand and walked her down the aisle to the vestibule to greet the two people who'd brought her beloved Stavros into the world.

While Stavros's father reached for him, his mother hugged Andrea. "You've made my son very happy," she said in a voice filled with tears. "I saw it in his face at the villa."

Andrea was so thrilled, she hugged her harder. "I'm going to try to make him happy forever. My mother died when I was born. I want us to be friends." By now, both of them were crying.

Stavros pulled her away. "Andrea? This is my father, Charis. I've wanted to introduce you for a long time."

The older man's eyes were a lighter gray than Stavros's, and they were moist with emotion. He had to clear his throat before he spoke. "It's an honor for me to meet the woman my son has chosen. He tells me you've saved his life and the company's reputation. I can't ask for more than that from a daughter-in-law. Welcome to the family."

Andrea smiled up at him. "I love him to the last breath in me. And I love you because you and your wife have raised the most marvelous son on earth."

Stavros put his arm around her waist and pressed her to his side. "There are no words to express how I really feel about you, Andrea," he whispered. "All I can do is show you." She didn't know how long they clung to each other before Leon reminded them other people were waiting.

They moved on to sign the wedding documents. Once that was done, Stavros walked her out into the hot noonday sun for pictures and congratulations.

Andrea's dad was the next person to hug her. His blue eyes twinkled. "You're Kyria Konstantinos now."

"I know. Can you believe it?"

"Stavros is getting the jewel in the crown, but I think he knows it by now."

"Dad—" She hugged him harder.

Leon butted in. "Save me some room. My brother is a lucky man." He kissed her on the cheek.

"Thank you, Leon. You don't know how much that means to me."

Then came his wife and children. They were followed by Theo and his family and Zander. Soon there was a crush of Stavros's relatives and friends, Raisa and her husband among them.

Suddenly she felt Stavros grab her around the waist. "Let's get back to the house. The sooner we feed our guests, the sooner we can leave on our honeymoon."

Leon drove them in a limo to the villa. A procession followed behind them, but Andrea was oblivious because Stavros was kissing the life out of her. She loved him so terribly and knew that his father's appearance had taken away the crushing pain of the past.

The first person Andrea hugged when they reached the house was Raisa. The housekeeper had spent several days preparing the wedding feast. Andrea had helped her with some of it.

A florist had come to fill the house with flowers. The villa was a showplace. Everyone marveled. Andrea was so proud of Stavros she could burst. He'd done all this and had accomplished so much in his life.

After many toasts and a lot of laughter, the wedding guests began to leave. While Stavros walked his parents out to Leon's limo, Andrea said goodbye to her father at the helicopter pad. He was flying to Thessaloniki, where he'd board a jet headed for the States.

Andrea was thankful for the privacy because she'd burst into tears with joy over Stavros's reconciliation with his father. "I'm so thankful he came, Dad."

"I am too, but don't forget that Stavros is going to need you more than ever."

"Thank heaven I have you. Thank you for my life, Dad. Thank you for everything you've done for me, everything that you are and stand for. Take care of yourself. Stavros says we'll fly to Denver next month to see you. I can't wait."

"Neither can I, honey. Love you." He gave her one more kiss before climbing into the helicopter.

She backed away to watch it take off and felt Stavros's arms encircle her waist. He waved to her father, then turned her around. "Guess what? Everyone's gone. Now it's just you and me. Let's hurry inside and change."

"You haven't told me where we're going tonight." Their bags were packed for a trip to Paris tomorrow.

A smile broke one corner of his compelling mouth. "You'll find out in a few minutes. I've been dreaming about it since the night we went searching for Darren."

He wanted to camp out with her! How did he know that was one of her secret desires?

They climbed the steps together. "I've been waiting to do this," he said and picked her up to carry her over the threshold. She didn't know how he did it while she was still in her wedding finery. He kissed her as he walked her through the house to the guest bedroom she'd been using. After he put her down, he undid the buttons on the back of her dress.

She felt him kiss the nape of her neck. His touch melted her.

"Hurry." He didn't have to tell her that. "Last person to the Jeep pays the penalty."

Andrea trembled with excitement as she stepped out of her dress. After laying it on the bed, she pulled a pair of shorts and a T-shirt out of the drawer and dressed in record time. After stepping into leather sandals, she raced through the house. But no matter how fast she'd been, Stavros had beaten her outside and was waiting in the Jeep wearing a crew-neck shirt and jeans.

"You cheated," she accused him.

He laughed hard and leaned across to give her a kiss. "I admit I changed out here."

"Where's your suit?"

"In the car."

"I hope you're not going to take a long time to find the right spot."

"Is my gorgeous wife nagging already?" he teased. Stavros started the engine and they were off down the road.

"Well, it *is* our honeymoon and I've never been on one before."

"Neither have I."

"I'm nervous."

"So am I."

"No, you're not."

"I've never been a husband before. I want everything to be perfect for us, Andrea."

"It already is because your father came and he loves you."

"Agreed."

"I have hopes of his coming to our first baby's christening."

"First?"

"Yes. I want your babies, darling. I told your mother I want us to be friends. She'll make the most wonderful grandmother. Honestly, Stavros, she's such a beauty it's no wonder you turned out like a Greek god."

He grinned. "I did?"

"My friendship with her is important to me."

"When she gets to know you better, she'll come to realize that the daughter she always wished she could have is my angel wife."

Tears trembled on her lashes. "Dad is crazy about you."

"I like him."

"He said those exact words to me about you before he walked me down the aisle. The ceremony was perfect."

"Short."

She chuckled. "I know traditional Greek weddings take hours. Thank you for sparing us that in this heat."

"The black sheep strikes again."

"Now that we're partners in crime we'll be known as Mr. and Mrs. Black Sheep."

He threw back his head in laughter.

It thrilled her that he sounded so happy.

"Did you know you looked like a vision coming down that aisle? I was so mesmerized I couldn't think."

"You weren't the only one in that condition. But I feel that way whenever I see you or sense your presence."

The night was exquisite as they drove through the scented pines. When he slowed down outside the village, it wasn't long before he found them the secluded spot where they'd spent another memorable night. He stopped the Jeep and turned off the engine.

"Would you believe me if I told you that the night we spent here the first time, I wanted it to be our wedding night."

"So did I," she whispered.

They climbed out of the Jeep and set up their little camp with the aid of the big flashlight.

"Oh—you bought a new sleeping bag!" Already her heart was pounding outrageously.

"Tonight we're doing this Italian-style. I measured this spot for our marriage bed to make sure it would hold two."

"You've outdone yourself, Figaro."

"So you like our bedroom."

"I adore it." She took off her sandals and climbed inside the bag. He could probably hear her heart thudding.

"Well, aren't you a brazen little hussy."

Andrea pulled the bag's edge up to her chin and looked out at him. "You already knew that about me when I asked if I could come with you to look for Darren. I figured that since you're going to wield a heavy penalty tonight, we might as well hurry and get this over with."

"Get what over with?" His voice sounded like silk as he turned off the flashlight and climbed in next to her.

"The thing the nuns talked to me about back in Venezuela."

"Like what?" He chuckled and pulled her into him to nuzzle her neck.

"Oh…just things."

"I'm not sure I know where to start."

"Don't drive me crazy, Stavros! I've been waiting for this all my life."

He started kissing her. "You mean this?"

"Yes."

"And this?"

"Y-yes."

"How about this?"

"Stavros!"

Andrea woke up several times during the night tangled in her husband's arms. Ecstasy like she'd never known had caused her to cling to him. He'd taught her a new language to speak. Eager for more, she started kissing him to wake him up so she could show him how fluent she was becoming. He responded with a husband's kiss, hot and consuming.

Oh, yes… Out of all the languages she'd learned, she liked this one best and intended to become an expert at it.

* * * * *

MILLS & BOON®
Hardback – March 2015

ROMANCE

The Taming of Xander Sterne	Carole Mortimer
In the Brazilian's Debt	Susan Stephens
At the Count's Bidding	Caitlin Crews
The Sheikh's Sinful Seduction	Dani Collins
The Real Romero	Cathy Williams
His Defiant Desert Queen	Jane Porter
Prince Nadir's Secret Heir	Michelle Conder
Princess's Secret Baby	Carol Marinelli
The Renegade Billionaire	Rebecca Winters
The Playboy of Rome	Jennifer Faye
Reunited with Her Italian Ex	Lucy Gordon
Her Knight in the Outback	Nikki Logan
Baby Twins to Bind Them	Carol Marinelli
The Firefighter to Heal Her Heart	Annie O'Neil
Thirty Days to Win His Wife	Andrea Laurence
Her Forbidden Cowboy	Charlene Sands
The Blackstone Heir	Dani Wade
After Hours with Her Ex	Maureen Child

MEDICAL

Tortured by Her Touch	Dianne Drake
It Happened in Vegas	Amy Ruttan
The Family She Needs	Sue MacKay
A Father for Poppy	Abigail Gordon

0215 GEN STD HB

MILLS & BOON®
Large Print – March 2015

ROMANCE

A Virgin for His Prize	Lucy Monroe
The Valquez Seduction	Melanie Milburne
Protecting the Desert Princess	Carol Marinelli
One Night with Morelli	Kim Lawrence
To Defy a Sheikh	Maisey Yates
The Russian's Acquisition	Dani Collins
The True King of Dahaar	Tara Pammi
The Twelve Dates of Christmas	Susan Meier
At the Chateau for Christmas	Rebecca Winters
A Very Special Holiday Gift	Barbara Hannay
A New Year Marriage Proposal	Kate Hardy

HISTORICAL

Darian Hunter: Duke of Desire	Carole Mortimer
Rescued by the Viscount	Anne Herries
The Rake's Bargain	Lucy Ashford
Unlaced by Candlelight	Various
The Warrior's Winter Bride	Denise Lynn

MEDICAL

A Secret Shared...	Marion Lennox
Flirting with the Doc of Her Dreams	Janice Lynn
The Doctor Who Made Her Love Again	Susan Carlisle
The Maverick Who Ruled Her Heart	Susan Carlisle
After One Forbidden Night...	Amber McKenzie
Dr Perfect on Her Doorstep	Lucy Clark

MILLS & BOON®
Hardback – April 2015

ROMANCE

The Billionaire's Bridal Bargain	Lynne Graham
At the Brazilian's Command	Susan Stephens
Carrying the Greek's Heir	Sharon Kendrick
The Sheikh's Princess Bride	Annie West
His Diamond of Convenience	Maisey Yates
Olivero's Outrageous Proposal	Kate Walker
The Italian's Deal for I Do	Jennifer Hayward
Virgin's Sweet Rebellion	Kate Hewitt
The Millionaire and the Maid	Michelle Douglas
Expecting the Earl's Baby	Jessica Gilmore
Best Man for the Bridesmaid	Jennifer Faye
It Started at a Wedding...	Kate Hardy
Just One Night?	Carol Marinelli
Meant-To-Be Family	Marion Lennox
The Soldier She Could Never Forget	Tina Beckett
The Doctor's Redemption	Susan Carlisle
Wanted: Parents for a Baby!	Laura Iding
His Perfect Bride?	Louisa Heaton
Twins on the Way	Janice Maynard
The Nanny Plan	Sarah M. Anderson

MILLS & BOON®
Large Print – April 2015

ROMANCE

Taken Over by the Billionaire	Miranda Lee
Christmas in Da Conti's Bed	Sharon Kendrick
His for Revenge	Caitlin Crews
A Rule Worth Breaking	Maggie Cox
What The Greek Wants Most	Maya Blake
The Magnate's Manifesto	Jennifer Hayward
To Claim His Heir by Christmas	Victoria Parker
Snowbound Surprise for the Billionaire	Michelle Douglas
Christmas Where They Belong	Marion Lennox
Meet Me Under the Mistletoe	Cara Colter
A Diamond in Her Stocking	Kandy Shepherd

HISTORICAL

Strangers at the Altar	Marguerite Kaye
Captured Countess	Ann Lethbridge
The Marquis's Awakening	Elizabeth Beacon
Innocent's Champion	Meriel Fuller
A Captain and a Rogue	Liz Tyner

MEDICAL

It Started with No Strings...	Kate Hardy
One More Night with Her Desert Prince...	Jennifer Taylor
Flirting with Dr Off-Limits	Robin Gianna
From Fling to Forever	Avril Tremayne
Dare She Date Again?	Amy Ruttan
The Surgeon's Christmas Wish	Annie O'Neil

MILLS & BOON®

Why shop at millsandboon.co.uk?

Each year, thousands of romance readers find their perfect read at millsandboon.co.uk. That's because we're passionate about bringing you the very best romantic fiction. Here are some of the advantages of shopping at www.millsandboon.co.uk:

* **Get new books first**—you'll be able to buy your favourite books one month before they hit the shops

* **Get exclusive discounts**—you'll also be able to buy our specially created monthly collections, with up to 50% off the RRP

* **Find your favourite authors**—latest news, interviews and new releases for all your favourite authors and series on our website, plus ideas for what to try next

* **Join in** —once you've bought your favourite books, don't forget to register with us to rate, review and join in the discussions

Visit **www.millsandboon.co.uk**
for all this and more today!